Also by SONNY BREWER

The Poet of Tolstoy Park

A Sound Like Thunder

BALLANTINE BOOKS

NEW YORK

A Sound Like Thunder

a novel

SONNY BREWER

A Sound Like Thunder is a work of fiction. Names, characters, places, and incidents are the products of the author's imagination or are used fictitiously. Any resemblance to actual events, locales, or persons, living or dead, is entirely coincidental.

Published in the United States by Ballantine Books, an imprint of The Random House Publishing Group, a division of Random House, Inc., New York.

BALLANTINE and colophon are registered trademarks of Random House, Inc.

LIBRARY OF CONGRESS CATALOGING-IN-PUBLICATION DATA

Brewer, Sonny.
A sound like thunder / Sonny Brewer.
p. cm.
ISBN 0-345-47633-6
1. World War, 1939–1945—Alabama—Fiction. 2. Fairhope (Ala.)—Fiction.
3. Domestic fiction. I. Title.
PS3602.R48S65 2006
813'.6—dc22 2005057100

Printed in the United States of America on acid-free paper

www.ballantinebooks.com

9 8 7 6 5 4 3 2 1

First Edition

Book design by Barbara M. Bachman

For Diana,

and Emily, and John Luke and Dylan,

for Nylene and Casey

—my foundation and my future

A Sound Like Thunder

I*t is a privilege,* this promontory of years—the heart grows looser and hurts are faster forgiven, the grip on grudges comes uncurled and things fall from view and we don't even look to see if a dust cloud is raised at our feet. Mostly we just ease on a farther piece down the road as if it did not matter what's back there. But the mind turns loose a little, too, as the years accrue near to that poetical-sounding fourscore peak from which, we know, the fall will soon come. So I will be forgiven, I'm sure, if I don't remember things with stunning clarity.

On this point, however, as I go reaching back, I'm quite certain I've got it right: There was a day, an actual day of the week, a Sunday, after which my father ceased any effort to hide his drinking. I would not remember the day if it weren't the day of the week traditionally set aside for our most holy thoughts and deeds, and I remember going to sleep that night nursing a crazy thought that my mother, Lillian, should make a note of this day along with all the other important family moments she'd jotted down on her Bible's front flyleaf.

Before that day, you could have asked me if Captain Dominus MacNee was a drinking man, and as you watched for signs of equivocation, I would have given a young son's disdainful flip of my head and a roll of my eyes and I would have said No.

And when you had been set aright and had walked away, I would have put my chin on my chest and squeezed my eyes shut and thought *Hell no. No glass bottle can put a boot on my daddy's neck.* Such was my indefatigable denial.

But after that day there was his bottle on the kitchen table. After that day there was his bottle on his desk near his inkwell. It was out on the porch in the shade of the big potted fern, and swinging in his hand as he walked out to the end of the dock at sunset. After that day he first swung his fist into my face.

Now I've let the edges go soft in my mind's pictures of Dominus and Lillian MacNee, and the sound of them calls to me more like a dove from a twilight juniper branch, now, than a belligerent jaybird squawking on a wire. It is right and a blessing of years for all things to mellow and fade.

So this is my tale. The imperfect recollections of Rover MacNee—scenes from that winter when I was a boy just turned sixteen. I'll help young Rove to see with the eyes I've got now, but I can tell you this: growing older only put colors inside the lines I drew way back then. And old men have permission to color outside the lines.

The pictures might look vaguely like scenes from *Summer of '42*, for me the quintessential coming-of-age flick. The cinematic pivot in my life's script, however, was in the winter. And it was 1941. Close, by a mile. And I don't come up with much humor in the emotional dynamics of my reluctant awakening. But I'll just roll it and we'll watch the dust motes float past that flickering light bouncing back from the broad and silver screen.

Often it seems out of focus. My old pal Bert, who is a retired Episcopal priest, tells me I should look up all references to eagles in the scriptures and see if I can divine— that's what he said, *divine*—any sense of a dream that repeats itself on the sleep-shaded screen of my mind. I don't think so. It's just a dream, I tell him, and as dreams go, pretty straightforward and not worth noticing except that it's always the same, always exactly the same. Let's say the scene is thirty-five miles north of Mobile, and the great bird sees far below him a wide river, wild at its banks. It is the five-mile run of the Alabama and the Tombigbee as one. His yellow eyes unblinking, the bald eagle pulls the wind through his exceptionally broad wings.

The river below him divides again into the Tensaw and the Mobile, and he flies on, scanning almost thirty miles of marshes, swamps, and prime rich bottomland thick with trees bearing ten thousand names. White feathers around the eagle's fierce eyes and powerfully curved beak ruffle in the thin air flowing around the hunter in his flight. He is a young male just at three feet in length from his diamond-hard beak to his ten-inch white tail feathers.

Beneath him sparkle ten thousand square miles of bays and bayous, creeks and lakes, and a riverine system that is called the Mobile-Tensaw Delta. He follows his south-by-southeast course and presently sees the first signs of man, marked in asphalt and rectangles now only five hundred feet below him. He banks to the west and drops another two hundred feet in seven seconds. His wings are extended in a glide, and he pulls a lazy arc to his left. Now at a hundred feet above the river he is flying north again.

A January wind whistles across the delta and waves the marsh grasses in dark ripples shaped like the shadowy ridges cut into dunes. It is cold and he is hungry. Both sensations quicken his senses and enliven him. His chest feels first the lift from the fresh, clean northerly breeze teasing him as he meets it, then a shudder courses out to his wingtip feathers, which sense each subtle shift in the air.

There!

Silvery shapes darting about just beneath the water's surface. He drops ten feet immediately, leveling, watching the fish below him. He is a loner, has not yet chosen his mate. This catch will be his alone.

His great curved talons flex, still held tightly to his body. His heart beats faster. His golden eye has picked its prey, and his entire body becomes a missile in free fall at a hundred and fifty miles an hour.

But then a brown blur explodes into the eagle's vision, and with an unfolding of wings and talons, the blur becomes an osprey plunging in for the kill at incredible speed. The osprey strikes a second before the eagle and steals the fish from underneath the outstretched legs and razor talons of the youngster.

Without a second's pause the regal bird of prey bends all his strength into his wings, and, unencumbered by the weight of a fish, quickly overtakes the osprey and surprises his competitor with a mighty thump from his chest. Once, twice, and the fish falls free. The eagle abandons the scuffle and follows the fish and snatches it up at the exact instant it strikes the river. He lifts his prey beneath him and resumes his flight, returning to the top branches of a lone cypress on a well-drained hummock a quarter mile back upriver.

The eagle will eat today.

Bert says he's absolutely sure that I *am* the eagle that I dream of, that it's not a symbol from which I can draw some long exegesis of the origin and meaning of Rove MacNee. If old Bert's right, then I've got it figured out that I am also this memory, these thoughts of me when I was a boy, thoughts that I fear will all too soon fly from my mind with ease.

Thunder, *low and trembling,* rolled across the breezeless bay, and I wondered from where I stood on the shaky wooden dock if the sheer weight of the sound could set tiny ripples in motion on the water's smooth face. The cypress two-by planking beneath my bare feet was weather-cracked and silvered. Many of the narrow wharf's rusting nails were loosened and backing out of the joists, allowing random boards to cup and twist, and the protruding nails to snag and bloody a boy's bare toes.

Gray dawn had not long since arisen, and my mother would be stirring the house to life, waking my younger brother, just turned ten. She would also awaken my grandmother, who had moved in with us soon after Grandpa Otis died.

My father was not at home, and the world was quiet.

Along this stretch of Alabama bayfront, no windows I could see were yet yellow with light, and I saw no one else moving. Ten or so miles to the north and west there on the other shore, across the smoky water the city of Mobile was still sleeping.

My father was captain of the *Mary Foster*, a fifty-foot melon schooner on a run to the New Basin Canal–front market out past Hagan Street in New Orleans. He was due back any day, maybe this morning, and usually drove home in his Ford truck from Farragut's Basin, where he kept the schooner at anchor. The captain called the basin Farragut's *Turn*, as did some of the older schoonermen, because it was the spot on Fish River where Admiral David Farragut, after the Civil War Battle of Mobile Bay, had found room enough to turn his gunboats around.

Sometimes, if the weather was fine, the captain would leave his truck at Farragut's and motor his broad skiff up the bay from the pass at Big Mouth, dropping off crew and deckhands at this or that fishing camp strung out down the bay. Now that I was sixteen and legal to drive, I would sometimes be sent back in the skiff to Farragut's to fetch home the truck, and I looked forward to those little excursions because I loved to drive. The run south down the bay alone in the skiff, my face skinning the wind and my hand twisting the throttle on the Evinrude, was almost as much fun.

My name is Rover, named for my father's beloved shining black Labrador retriever that drowned in the wind-tossed waves of Mobile Bay while chasing a wounded mallard. The dog had paddled madly and happily, one might guess, after the duck through the frothy chop until he sank in exhaustion in five feet of brackish water not a hundred yards offshore from our bayside cottage the day before I was born.

The captain, in naming his son after his dog, had revealed a sense of humor that I had failed to inherit. I came up short of laughing each time I fought this or that taunting schoolmate who called me Rover. On my first day of school, I had dropped the last "r" and given my name as Rove, a name I did not mind actually. Anyone who added back the "r" and addressed me so had a fight on his hands. Years later David MacFarland would lift his upper lip with his index finger and show me a chipped tooth, would turn loose his lip, and let it segue into a smile and tell me parents should be more careful what they name their kids. We were fourteen when I punched him in the mouth. I walked away with a torn knuckle on my right hand, a scar to match David's chip.

With this weather building, my father would drive instead of motoring up the bay in the skiff. Even knowing that, I looked south down the bay. I saw no skiff. I let my eyes sweep the horizon and a steam passenger ferry, an elongated black shape some miles across the flat water, was trailing a thin tendril of smoke into the dull pewter sky. It was the only thing moving on Mobile Bay as far as I could see. I lifted my shoulders against a cold shiver starting down my neck. The November morning still held the chill from last night's low temperature which had dipped to near forty degrees.

It would storm today. This odd stillness would soon be shattered, rough weather probably setting in before the *Bay Queen* made the dock at Stedman's Landing, three or so miles up the shore north of Fairhope. If I did not hurry home I might get caught in the rain, which, in fact, I did not mind. But, on the other hand, if I did not hurry, there was some chance that my father would be already seated at the kitchen table. I did not want to come into the house after him.

My preference, in fact, if it were not for leaving Mother alone to deal with the captain, would be to stay away entirely.

I had worked the deck on the *Mary Foster,* and I knew that when the captain sailed home, done with the white-shirted dealers in New Orleans who had haggled down his prices, done with the sweating thick-armed roustabouts who off-loaded the fat, striped melons—or in other seasons sweet potatoes or turpentine or what have you—and when his crew had piled them onto waiting trucks, when the captain had heeled to breezes across Lake Pontchartrain, negotiated the currents in the pass at the Rigolets and into Lake Borgne, laid down the lee rail in gusts across the Mississippi Sound, ghosted past Dauphin Island and Fort Gaines to starboard and made his cut northward into Mobile Bay with Fort Morgan off his stern quarter, when he had pointed the bow of the *Mary Foster* east into the narrow mouth of Weeks Bay, then slid the schooner between Fish River's twisty and wooded banks, bending around curve after curve those short four miles upstream to Farragut's Basin, when he had anchored there with the rest of the schooner fleet, then the good captain was ready for a bottle of Scotch whisky.

I also knew, because I overheard the accusations from Mother and heard no attendant denial from my father, that the captain sometimes carried on with Creole whores at Lanaux's Landing in Magnolia Springs, and lay out drunk for several days instead of coming home when the *Mary Foster* returned to port. And when he'd had a sailor's fill of this merriment, the captain would drive through the farmlands rattling along Baldwin County back roads to our home south of Fairhope near Battles Wharf. Captain Dominus MacNee's homecomings were usually at the breakfast hour; they were usually noisy and threatening.

In the last two years, that long since the captain seemed to have stepped into an abyss and dragged himself out another man entirely, I had grown to sometimes hate for my father to come home, and sometimes secretly wished he would drown at sea. I believed there was at least some chance it might happen. And nights in my dream-rumpled bed, when that bad thing had there in the dark come to pass, I would awaken in tears already missing him.

Because my father might be coming home this morning, and because a profaning drunk at the breakfast table would be enough for Mother to manage without wondering after my whereabouts, and because I wished for the small advantage I might gain from being first ahead of the captain in Mother's kitchen, I thought I might better get on home. I should coil my cast net down into the galvanized bucket beside my bare feet on the dock, take up its bail, and begin walking down the bluff overlooking the bay toward home.

It was enough of a hardship on my mother that my grandmother was sickly, and enough for her to get my reluctant brother Julian moving in the morning. I should start now walking that way, and then there crossed the plain of my mind a shadow, something wheeling high up and indistinguishable, but bearing some likeness to pain. So I stood stock-still and looked out across the water's surface, settling my mind into something real, and letting my imaginings slip away.

I hung my toes off the boards and leaned out, my palms on my knees, and looked down into the water, and if I thought I might have spied some fish backs passing under the dock, I was wrong and saw only myself looking up at me. My grandmother told me I was wide-shouldered and straight-backed like my father, but my bent-over silhouette didn't reflect that, couldn't show that I was just a little taller than most of the boys in my class. Mostly what I saw was an indistinct face and some pretty wild hair going this way and that. You couldn't tell from the wavy picture the water gave back to me that my hair was the color of wheat straw, or that my eyes were blue. You couldn't tell that my thoughts were still tearing this way and that like cats before a slobbering loudmouthed hound.

When my father shipped out days ago, he'd been quiet, and his eyes hard. He had not spoken a word to me or to Mother on his way out the kitchen door, and I had no reason to hope that the storm under his sailor's cap had blown over. It would be what it would be, and it would be that soon.

I stood up, turned, and got my sixteen-foot cast net and caught it up and looped it in my left hand like a cowboy's lariat, with the lead line bound to my wrist there. The morning sun was just topping the tree line back of the beach, and I turned my face into that revealing light, my eyes daring the sun. I didn't blink. I ran my fingers through my hair as if to comb it for the guest coming up through the trees.

The full lower skirt of the net with its leaded hem was draped over my right shoulder. My blue cotton shirt was soaked back and front from repeated tosses and retrievals of the net and I smelled fishy, though not one fish had found my net. I wondered, if a stranger came up on me, would he have judged, in that quick way we do, that he liked me? Or would I stand a better chance for a good first impression coming out the church door with a dry shirt tucked into my trousers and shoes on my feet? I wondered what made me care one way or the other. A fight or a standoff could be just as meaningful as uninformed positive regard. But there was no one about, and I heard only gulls laughing far off, and, closer, the splashing dive of a pelican.

The briny smell of the cold, brackish water seemed set

into my wet skin and hair. My bucket was empty. Not a single mullet glass-eyed the sky from its bottom. One last toss and I would go.

I did not expect to catch a fish this morning, but it didn't matter. It was the toss of the net, not the catch in the bucket that drew me out into the dark before dawn to this wobbly dock. Three, four mornings out of a week lately found me at Walcott's pier, barefoot in any weather, ready with my net to spin it in a perfect circle out over the water ten feet below at the slight silver shimmer of a fat mullet lazing past underneath. I liked this dock because it stood so high above the surface of the bay. Mr. Walcott, when I first asked last year, had told me I could use the dock anytime. And in months of afternoons after school that lasted until dusk, of long Saturdays and Sundays after church, and, in the last several weeks, mornings at daybreak, I had learned to toss my net as my grandfather had promised I would.

"Here, Rove, I'm just going to show you the basics," my grandfather had said. "Throwing a mullet net is like writing your name. You'll come up with your own way of doing it that won't be exactly like anybody else's." And so the finer techniques, I was told, would come after I'd "wasted" lots of time on the Big Pier on the bay at the foot of the hill below town.

When I had failed time after time to get the net to do what I wanted, and said to my grandfather that I thought I'd just stick to a hook and a line, my grandfather shook his head. "Aw, you don't need a barb, boy! No, you are like

Peter the Fisherman with his nets. I promise you, son, you just are not holding your mouth right." And the old man had made me go with him and spend half a day mending a tattered net, which he then gave to me. It was the net I still used on that morning, and I wish I had it still.

Yellowed and curling photographs of Grandpa Otis still invoke in me a sense of loss, or more, as if I'd been cheated of the company of a grandfather who should have been there for me as long as I needed him. The time I did have with him he completely fulfilled for me the archetype of a grandfather that a growing boy needs. Grandpa Otis was the patriarch and kin-keeper in my family, and without him I, for one, often felt cut loose and adrift.

My father's father, John Frank, never came close to setting the family anchor and seemed to me, as a child, rough and brittle and unyielding, like a knobby stick draped with a man's clothing. In Granny Wooten's husband, however, from one particular oval frame of carved mahogany, I saw my own eyes, my own face looking back at me: Robert Otis Wooten bestowed upon me in benign generosity his straight nose and broad forehead, his tumble of unbrushable yellow-blond hair. The sepia tint of the paper behind the glass didn't convey the color of his eyes, but they were blue. Granny Wooten told me time and again after he died that I had her Otis's eyes.

Many times I wondered if it was he, not the captain, who'd passed along to me my strong back and strong arms. I saw Grandpa Otis wrestle a hundred pounds onto his shoulder without a sound. Some men I've known could carry their heavy end of a load only with a grunt or a growl. I will always think of him as being strong like a bull, silent as the night. With blue eyes. Like me.

Fairhope's municipal pier, the Big Pier, jutting almost due west a quarter mile into Mobile Bay, was in 1941 a place for steam ferryboats and gaff-rigged sailboats to dock, for townspeople to gather and stroll, maybe to music from a loud-speaker on a pole, maybe the tunes of Benny Goodman, or Duke Ellington, or the Andrews Sisters. Maybe the strollers had just come down the hill to the bay from in front of their parlor radios and Kate Smith's rendition of "God Bless America," and the song still played in their heads, and maybe Kate's sweet voice calmed the jitters they caught from newspaper headlines that rumbled about the war in Europe.

The Big Pier's finger docks were diving and jumping platforms for swimmers. The Big Pier was a wharf for fishermen to trail heavy lines into the waves, and a high spot for net casters to float their spidery webs downward over the rails, falling like moonlight onto the water, only now and again netting shiny-sided fish. I spent hours in the sun just watching: how one made his coils with the net on the retrieval, how another divided the net's skirt into some in this hand and some over the shoulder, how yet another made a waltz-like turn at the rail to send his net flying.

And I tried this and that technique. With countless throws, I finally grew more skillful and more certain of what would become of the net when I let it leave my hand. A scant few well-thrown nets in the first hundred tries became a dozen or more good tosses in the second hundred tries. And so on until I discovered that when my net opened into a complete wide circle, when it arced downward as round as a silver dollar and swished into the water with its lead hem defining my good toss with a neat "o" and a tiny sizzle of bubbles, I did not care in the least that a fish might be caught there in my net. To take a bundled net, all a-dangle from my arm and shoulder, and to rise on the balls of my feet and let it fly with a measured whirl of my body, and have my net spin out into the air round as an iris . . . well, I found this as satisfying as the last big sigh before falling asleep on cool sheets.

G*randpa Otis said* that to catch mullet in a net you must hold your mouth right. But what came from my mouth when I landed my first net full to bursting with flopping silver-scaled mullets didn't pass through lips held right, I think. Grandpa Otis, had he still been alive to hear me, or had he heard tell of my cursing that day, would have given me a good-natured knock on the head.

And it would have been Julian, who sat cross-legged on the dock behind me when I hauled in my net, who'd run to Grandpa Otis and snitch on me for saying bad words, fulfilling the function of a younger brother. Julian never accused me of anything to our father, did not seek that unpredictable audience, but Julian might have also ratted on me to Mother. He would try anything to have the stage with her, if only for a moment. She never had the same eyes for her second son that she had for me. Julian the Parenthetical. I stood in the full light of Mother's smiling favor while Julian lurked in the outer dark, his dusty cheeks tracking un-wiped tears.

And I would, if I could, confess it out of my soul that I, too, left my brother on the periphery. I do not recall ever once tossing a baseball with him, but, worse, I cannot re-member listening to him, holding his eyes, when he might have needed only that from me. It was almost too late, years later, when I admitted I had no real background with Julian. The sibling landscape was flat, there was not a hill punched up or a gully carved out by the blood-in-the-eye meanness that brothers ought to share, not a turning, flowing stream or patch of bending grass fed by the vigor-ous, sappy goodness that sticks brothers together until they're old men.

But Grandpa Otis had already passed from us the morning I caught the load of mullet, so Julian missed a chance to make a little crater that we could have laughed over together years later.

Even if I'd been knocked on the head a bit at just that moment, I would not have cared. I didn't even have to tug on the line to know I'd let my net down on an entire school of mullet. I felt the vibration hum up into my fin-gers within seconds of watching it disappear with a *shish* into the water under Walcott's dock. The vibrations turned into bumps and quivers running along the lead line. I do believe I could have hoisted the catch onto the dock by myself, but Julian danced and hooted and curled and un-curled his hands impatient to help me haul up the line. I made him promise to help me gut and scale the fish. Julian would have jumped into a tangle of stinging jellyfish if I'd asked him.

While he agreed with nods and grunts and promises to help me, his eyes never left the point where my lead line disappeared beneath the reflecting water. I turned at an angle to let him get his hands on the line with mine. And we pulled and laughed and lifted until the bulging net thudded onto the dock. Never shall I forget the number of mullet we took home to clean and hickory-smoke: nineteen! A jubilee on a single cast of my net. And smoked mullet fillets for a month. Julian would later speak of that catch like some soldiers regale barbershop patrons with a hill taken under fire.

I could not wait, myself, to apprise Father Brown of my Gospel story–size bounty. *Be ye fishers of men* was not lost on him, but I'm not sure he bore true witness to the order of his priorities when he said to me, "First, I love the pulpit, Rove. Followed closely by hanging around the docks." He lifted his arms in a pontifical gesture, his net hanging wet on his shoulders.

"They might as well be the apostles, son," Father Brown continued, "those yellow-slickered men telling tales of boats and fishes, and sailors going on about hurricanes and windward legs and sunset coves. The more time you spend in sight of these sailing sloops and working boats, listening for some salty old sea buzzard's story, the closer to God you'll be, Rove. Don't forget it."

And how could I or anybody living along the coastal crescent extending inland only some fifty miles or so from

the Gulf of Mexico—or writ larger, the entire coastal rim
of our country—how could you fail to feel the connection
of the water's spirit? At less than fifty miles inland there's
an invisible saltwater line where you pass into the realm of
the hinterlands. The sea gives up its ghost and cannot be
felt in the marrow.

The mind of an inlander might conjure images of
whitecaps and sand, of masts and bowsprits, might think
it hears halyards slapping and the whisper of a fresh
northerly through palmetto scrub, might even be tempted
to believe it catches the scent of brine and fish blood, but
it is only a shadow. The real thing is closer to the sun. A
soft-shell crab battered with flour and spices and fried in
popping-hot oil can be put on a table in Memphis, Ten-
nessee. But, it is not as delightful on the tongue as in Mobile or New Orleans.

Father Brown was the priest at Sacred Heart Catholic
Church in Battles Wharf, and a friend of my father, and a
dismayed watcher of the change in the captain as he
turned more and more to the bottle. The priest was also
the son of a son of a sailor, both Mobile Bay bar pilots,
but took to the sanctified cloth of the priesthood rather
than the heavy canvas of a well-sewn mainsail. Still, he
had salt-water in his veins enough to brindle his black hair
and beard with equal amounts of gray, and him just forty
or so.

And the priest and my father, the captain, were fast
friends, though my father rarely darkened the door of any
church. Not Father Brown's, nor the church of my family,

Saint James' Episcopal. So I can guess that the captain never sought counsel nor consolation from the preachers in town, never looked to the men in the pulpits for help to fight his devils. Dominus MacNee's life and the slings and arrows of his outrageous fortunes were suffered by him alone. Until he passed them along to the people at arm's length.

I *guessed at the time.* Maybe a little before six. The light was growing in the east. One more toss of my net. Too much thinking had spoiled the last toss. Not enough intuition, not enough instinctive motion had guided me, and my net had struck the water in the shape of a banana. I was tired and my muscles were tense. I purposefully eased my shoulders, let my mind slip past my father, past my mother, past my brother and grandmother, to feel only the wet weave of the net in my hand, to sense only the water trickling down my chest underneath my shirt, the chill on my skin, to see only the syrupy undulations of the smooth bay, to hear only the distant roll of thunder, and I made my toss. The net flew like a whisper and spread evenly and round and I knew before it hit the water that it was a perfect throw, and one good for leaving.

I gave a tug on my net, felt no fish tremble in the mesh down in the dark water, and drew in the net and coiled it into my bucket. Before taking up the net and bucket, I turned up my shirt collar and buttoned the top button. I huffed out a big breath and watched it gather like a small cloud, hanging briefly in the chilly, windless morning. The yellow lights in Mother's kitchen would be welcome, the delicious scent of her baking biscuits a treat to see me home. And if my father was not there, a small prayer would be answered.

I made my way, swinging my bucket slowly and with my collar up and my face down, under the tall pines and moss-draped live oaks in the growing morning light falling on the path. I walked under tall pines along the well-worn footpath that led along the bay and down a slope to where a copse of ragged cypress trees stood guard over a small shallow pool washed out in the sand. The beach along here was narrow, and tangles of pine tree roots were undercut by the sloshing of incoming waves. I offered my big toe to a fiddler crab but it skittered to cover behind a piece of driftwood.

I'd be home in five minutes, to the Creole cottage set on the bluff under mossy old-growth oaks and pines, sweet bay and magnolias, and standing back fifty yards from the beach. The oyster-shell road running parallel to the shoreline into Fairhope was another hundred yards behind the house. This place I knew as home had been called Magnolia Bayhouse for three generations of MacNees. My father, the captain, got title to the property when his father, John Frank MacNee, died in 1929.

John Frank's father, Patrick William, also a captain—a Mobile Bay bar pilot—had built the roomy cottage in 1840 in the shade of a massive, gnarly magnolia. The exterior was white-painted cypress board-and-batten siding with green shuttered ten-foot-tall windows. A high-pitched cedar shake roof covered the cottage proper, and a screened gallery its full width was set with an array of chairs and rockers and settees positioned for watching sunsets paint the evening sky and anvil-gray storms march across the bay.

A fresh breeze could brush and sway the heavy draperies of Spanish moss in the tree branches and waxy green leaves and make such a hissing reproach that even children would sometimes stop their playing and look, almost reverently, upward into the flexing gray-barked limbs as though awaiting permission to make another move or another sound.

I had been up since 4:30 and had not slept well during the night. My grandmother's soft breathing in the next bedroom would at times grow loud and wet and she would cough for a brief spell and when the racking had stopped she would sigh, but more like a wavering moan. Granny Wooten was not well, and I was distressed by my helplessness to offer her comfort.

How many times had she tended some wound of mine—a rusty nail in my foot, a scraped elbow, a bee sting; how many times had she soothed my fevered forehead with a damp cloth, made some poultice for an aching molar? The sounds she made in the night last night had kept me from sleeping soundly, and I'd arisen tired. My morning's walk to Walcott's pier had not been the blood-stirring wakeup I typically enjoyed.

I *knew for certain* my grandmother was dying, though no such thing was prophesied on the premises of Magnolia Bayhouse, and, on the contrary, my mother specifically denied it. She yelled at Julian when he ventured, "Is Gran Gran fixing to die?"

Nor did I want to face her passing. My grandmother mothered me in ways Lillian MacNee did not: told me about books and put them into my hands; asked me to think about poems she'd read aloud to me, and asked me what was the thought behind a quatrain; gave me a small black-backed journal and asked me to try my hand at rhyming lines that told a story, or asked me to go sit out on the porch and write two paragraphs, or three, describing what I saw. She used big words with a wink, and a nod toward the *Webster's*. Plus, she stirred up in me, just from her company, an intense fondness. It was not that she "raised" me, as we say. It was that she got down to the heart of me and was so easy to love.

And the reading. She was such a good teacher. Granny Wooten did not teach me to read, not literally. Teachers at the schoolhouse did that. My mother helped me at the kitchen table. But Granny Wooten handed me the right book at the right time, conjuring peculiar magic, books that arrested so completely my woodpecker-like tapping at a thousand notions, tree to tree to tree from hill to holler.

How did that old woman know it would be Mark Twain I would take to, and not, say, Jack London? After all, I've still got my copy of London's *Tales of the Fish Patrol.* Who could have faulted Granny Wooten if she'd picked that book with its account of a boy, sixteen, chasing all over San Francisco Bay in his little sloop *Reindeer?* It would have been a safe bet that a boy (and I myself was a sailing boy at that) would like to read about another boy who was an actual deputy patrolman for the Fish Commission. And I can say for certain that, even in view of my later affection for Jack London, he could not have twisted my arm the way Twain did when Twain grabbed hold of me with *The Adventures of Huckleberry Finn.* Granny Wooten knew the book would work for me.

Indeed, she herself *worked* for me. Maybe saved my life. And so I didn't want to hear Julian's talk about Gran Gran, but I remember thinking, *Granny Wooten is dying.* I'd been watching her go down since Mother had brought her to live with us a month or so after my grandfather died. With Grandpa Otis gone, she seemed drained and tired all the time. My mother said such was not uncommon, but that she would recover in time. And she did, became a good copy of her feisty self again within a year.

But then when the Lawtons bought her place, she became blue and ill-tempered again. She began to "take sick" as she called it, and I do believe that she did just that: took the sickness unto herself, albeit without the guilty knowledge that she was doing so. I, for one, began to think she would not hold on for much longer.

I can recall when I sat down with her in the parlor that day that the season's first good northerly had swept in the night before and cleared away all the haze and I could see the western shore of Mobile Bay like it was spread there between my outstretched left and right palms. Just right there. When I had had enough of scanning the horizon, had come into the house off the front porch, and sat down with her that day, Granny Wooten had leaned her head on my shoulder and patted my knee and called me Otis. All she said was, Otis, and waited for a while and said, "It has been a long, good walk. I am so tired. Are you tired, Otis?" And she waited for another bit, then said, "I thought you might be; well, soon enough now." And she went to sleep with her hand on my knee. I didn't want to stir and awaken her, even when I felt spittle from her open mouth forming a wet spot on my shirt.

I knew I would miss Granny Wooten when she died. But I wouldn't have wanted to hold her back from the rest she needed. I remember that I sometimes got tired, too, but I was sixteen then and just starting out and I would have a long way to go to catch up with her.

A *flash in the bunched* low clouds off to the west, and the air seemed to split as deep thunder pounded the earth again. So insistent, I thought, so taunting. I had almost covered the last of the remaining steps to our house before the first big raindrops thunked the ground. There came another sonorous roll so low and pulsing it almost hurt my eardrums. I'd slowed to an easy pace, but a chilly gust bumped me and I turned to see a heavy curtain of rain a half mile offshore, quickly sliding my way. Goose bumps peppered my arms and I trotted the last few yards to the covered gallery extending across the front of our house.

I put my net bucket on the ground beside the newel post at the porch steps, laid a short piece of cypress board over the top of the bucket so the net would not soak in rainwater, and mounted the few treads. I padded to the front door and took the doorknob and gave it a twist, half expecting to find the door ajar. I was relieved that it was still shut, but surprised that no lights were on and the house still quiet.

I went inside, down the hall, choosing not to turn on lights as I passed the switches. My footsteps emphasized the quietness of the house. I was beginning to feel stirrings of anxiety as I drew farther into the silence, and then I suddenly remembered that there was no school today and no reason for my family to be up yet. Tomorrow was Thanksgiving Day, a new national holiday. The quiet also meant my father was not home, and for that I relaxed, let my breath ease out.

I stood quietly looking through the open door of my father's study into the darkness there that smelled of pipe smoke and listened as the steady *tick-tock-tick-tock* of the manteltop clock reached into the quiet spaces of the house. I went into the study and there turned on a single lamp on the captain's desk and with a soft click a pool of light warmed the varnished oak surface and the blotter and the cup of sharpened pencils and a stack of lined notebook pages arranged beside my father's fountain pen in its holder. One of his many pipes lay in an ashtray beside a pouch of aromatic tobacco, a scent that lingered in the room like a ghost of my father. A tilted, standing photograph of a young woman, my mother, Lillian, smiled at me from the corner of Father's desk.

I had not seen that smile on my mother's face in some time. I knew she was worried about Granny Wooten, though she denied that anything was wrong with her mother. And so it seemed in the everyday of things that

Mother was locked into some immobility of real emotions, as if the best of her smiles had been appropriated by the cameras snapping at her when she was a younger woman. She was now in her thirties, still pretty, but more matriarchal than "melting and sensuous," as I remembered Theodore Dreiser's description of that second stage of a woman's metamorphosis. Mother's eyes were a soft gray, almost blue, and set against her tanned face and dark brown hair, the effect was arresting. She was not as tall as me, but her graceful motion and upright bearing gave her an advantage even in a crowded room.

Granny Wooten said that a woman is four separate creatures in her life: first a girl, then a young woman *capable* of having children, which is not the same as the woman who has borne a son or daughter, and then when her children have themselves had children she is a grandmother, and yet a different woman. On the other hand, she suggested that men are simply larger versions of themselves as boys. And they have different toys, some of which are dangerous.

In my mother's third stage—if we buy my grandmother's thinking, when Lillian MacNee's skin remembered her former self as the object of men's desire, and yearned after the shiver a man's hand brought to the nape of her neck—I happened down to the beach to find her swimming nude. I was ten. She was twenty yards out, taking long, silent strokes and drawing quickly to the beach. She didn't see me until she was standing in water to her knees. I was transfixed, stood there motionless and fascinated. Her beauty drifted over me like a dream of free flight, and she walked up on the beach and slipped into her loose cotton dress before saying a word.

"Your father once gazed at me with such astonishment," she said. I had no idea, then, of what she spoke. But I remembered what she said and years later when I recalled her voice I heard there the wistfulness that I missed that day on the beach.

I looked at the picture of my lovely mother as I sat down in the captain's swivel chair and drew up closer to the desk. I had now and again ventured into this room, had read many of Father's books, and each time I sat at the captain's desk and looked around the room, at the books on the rows of shelves, the framed charts on the walls, the art and miscellaneous keepsakes—his toys—I wondered who was the man I called Father.

It must be true, what I'd read in that essay of Emerson's— indeed, from that very book on the fourth shelf up there. I had one day noticed the red ribbon dangling over the spine of the Emerson, had taken down the book, and discovered a passage underlined by Captain MacNee. What the son of the captain, I, the true son of a son of a sailor, what I read there in the essay called "Spiritual Laws" was that a man is "a selecting principle, gathering his like to him, wherever he goes . . . like one of those booms which are set out from the shore on rivers to catch drift-wood. . . . What attracts my attention shall have it," said Emerson. "The soul's emphasis is always right."

Still, I could not discern from this assortment collected

according to the emphasis of my father's soul much about the man's dreams and fears, and allowed that Granny Wooten was probably right, that I would come to see my father more clearly only with each of my own passing years. But I thought that the benefit from such seeing would be left farther and farther behind. What difference would it make to solve the riddle of my father when I was no longer a son in my father's house?

There again, the thunder. A booming initial report that reverberated in the walls of the small office, and a vibrating moan that echoed after and traveled through the tongue-and-groove hickory floorboards and tingled the tendons of my feet and the muscles in my calves.

The door opened without a knock, but with a rattling of the knob, and swung fast into the room and banged back against the bookcases built into the walls opposite the desk. I flinched. The early-morning light flickered outside the tall window with the lightning's jittery play in the clouds that hung lower and lower as my father hard-booted into the study. The captain sidestepped the mutt that dashed in past him. It was the neighbor's patchwork-colored dog, the mixed breed they called Elberta.

Even with the crazy little dog crashing into the room, I could not take my eyes off Father, who had not removed his cap, one of those dark woolen, billed caps known as a Greek sailor's cap. My father's face was dark with a short stubble of salt-and-pepper beard.

"Rove, what are you doing in here?" The captain's eyes were hard and unyielding as metal bearings.

I was nine when the captain brought a dog home for me. It was an Airedale terrier, and to me he was the most beautiful dog in the world with his tangled coat the color of old leather. My mother said she'd never seen an uglier, smellier dog and was terrified of him, mostly after my father's long story about how Badger was trained to fight one-on-one against bears or lions, and to kill them with ripping bites—that's what he'd said, *ripping*—to the neck or the gut.

When I was fourteen something got wrong with Badger's back and he grew unable to walk. Badger holed up underneath Magnolia Bayhouse and would eat only when I'd crawl under the house and feed him by hand.

My father made me watch while he shot Badger with a pistol. He said it was what you do to lame dogs.

The father who gave him to me would have done the very same thing, but would not have allowed me to see him do it. And I don't think he would have made me bury my dog. But the father of the whiskey days said that the boy who fed him should also bury him. And his eyes left no question that he meant for me to do just that.

Even carrying Badger to the hole I dug, he didn't smell bad. He only smelled like a dog.

I *had not yet answered* my father's question. I did not know what to say, couldn't think of a simple reason why I sat in his chair. "I'm sitting here trying to catch a glimpse of my father" would probably not be well received. My chest tightened with each second's delay.

Still, somehow, I slipped away from the threat of the moment, only for the space of a breath, and in that brief interlude a smile sprang to my lips. Elberta's claws lost purchase on the polished boards and her legs splayed out and her hindquarters dropped to the floor as she spun sideways trying to get to her feet and into the small space underneath the desk.

Fishing for a reply where there was not one, I lacked the presence of mind to simply push back my father's chair and stand up, and while I paused, the whining, crying mutt brushed my leg and ducked under the desk at my feet. She was now so far back into the recess there that I, had I been willing to try, could not have reached the mutt to pat her head, to calm her down.

"Damn mangy cur!" the captain said. "Little beast nearly knocked me down."

My father actually seemed to have forgotten me and headed past his desk, rounding it with his eyes down, his neck craned like he meant to find the dog. The scowl on his face said he'd grab her by the scruff of her neck, should he get his hands on her, and fling her out into the stormy morning. I got up from the desk and out of the way quickly.

The intermittent heavy drops of rain tapping against the tin roof on the cottage suddenly grew into a loud and evenly drumming complaint. On other days, I had watched just such a blanketing rain seem to smother the wind and knock down smaller waves out in the bay. And the nervous ripples on the water, as from cat's paws playfully clawing the backs of the gray swells, would disappear before such a shushing rain. Today, the rain had no quieting effect.

"Dominus MacNee, you stop right there." My mother's voice hardly rose. One might have thought it teasing. She stood in the doorway to the captain's study, pulling her worn cotton robe closed and tying the sash about her waist. That done, she lifted her hands and brushed back away from her cheeks thick strands of hair, tucking them into the bun that she loosely coiled about her head each night before bed. The edge of authority in Mother's voice was as plain and unmistakable as the reverend Harvey

Jones's from his Sunday morning pulpit at Saint James' Church.

Mother stiffened her spine and stood upright. She was silhouetted by the bulb she'd switched on in the hall. I did not make to rise, and my eyes found and held desperately the eyes of my mother from within the brown shadow obscuring her face. The captain stopped, the incredulity on his face transformed into a narrowing of his eyes. He conveyed something more like outright contempt for this woman who dared to give him an order.

"The neighbor should take better care to keep up his dog. I will not have it careening about in my study, and my pistol will damn well agree," my father said, his teeth slightly bared like a canine adversary of the tiny wiry-haired mutt huddled and keening at my feet.

"Dominus"—Mother became quickly coquettish—"have you completely forgotten the good manners you once easily practiced in my presence?" She smiled at her husband, took only a single step nearer to him and stood, and put both hands on her hips. My father was now beside his desk. Perhaps it was the whiskey, perhaps nights without sleep, but the captain was clearly being robbed of his command here in this his own room, in this his own house.

Mother was managing him this time. I had seen her take this very same tack before and had seen the strategy fail. On other mornings just such as this, I had seen all hell break loose when Mother attempted to head off the captain's foul mood or bad behavior.

"Men, my dear," the captain said, regaining some of his swagger, "will stop at no pretense when they are courting a woman." He made little effort to conceal a wry smile that implied that she must know, too, how things change when the courtship is over and the prize has been won, when time and familiarity have dulled infatuation's sparkle.

I could not reconcile how easily this man and woman had fooled the record when they stood before a distant afternoon's camera with their arms entwined, leaning against a long-fendered shiny black car. The silver-framed black-and-white photograph now hanging in the parlor belied these awful fights of late.

I watched Mother glance at the floor underneath the captain's desk. When I looked there myself I could see one mottled white-and-brown paw extended into the light from the shadowy hiding place. Mother shook her head and smiled. "Silly little dog."

I knew that both my mother and I were equally glad for Elberta's ad-lib appearance, her welcome counterpoint.

"Troublesome mutt," Father corrected. "Cowardly cur almost unhinged my door." I watched as the dog withdrew its paw into the shadow, and considered getting it out of there, but thought Elberta might kick up some kind of fuss and get into bigger trouble.

Mother said, "Well, Dominus, you are home and we shall not spoil the start of a day either talking about or fooling with skittish dogs."

My mother turned to me.

"Rove, take that dog onto the porch, please. It can sit

there until the rain stops, then it will surely go home. And wake up your brother, then see about your grandmother. Just look in on her. I'll get her up when I have breakfast on the table."

I pushed back the desk chair and bent down and dragged the squirming dog into my arms, then stood up to go. It was, to me, quite a feat that my mother could step into the path of my father and wave him off his course, have him take in his sails and slow down. Still, I stepped well clear of the captain, and, in fact, made no eye contact with my mother or my father.

At the door, I looked back briefly. Father had already sat down at his desk, put his elbows on the brown leather desk pad, and laced his fingers to make a teepee of his forearms. Behind his clasped hands, he looked like he might be praying, or defending his face from an attacker. I was sure, now, that this man and this woman were playing out their unhappiness in different ways. But he was Captain Dominus MacNee and she was Miss Lillian, and I believed neither would ever discover whether each was the other's pain, or whether they might again someday lean together on some shiny black fender and save each other.

I was hardly three steps down the hall, with Elberta trembling against my chest, when Mother's voice, now gone hard and loud, reached me: "Dominus, my mother is very sick. She has been asking for you for three days. Your ship docked two days ago."

"How do you know when my ship docked, Lillian, dear?"

I stopped and stroked the dog's muzzle so it would be quiet. I turned my head, inclining my ear back down the hall toward the study.

"Do you think your deckhands all go to that devilish place in Magnolia Springs?" my mother asked, all the calm now gone from her voice. "Some have families, Dominus, and come straight home when their ship is at anchor. Some of your men may even be seen in the store buying things for their families and home."

I guessed my mother would pause with this implication, but she charged right on, and perhaps that was the better way with the captain. It would be a bigger risk for her to go fawning about with him when his head was ragged from three days of drinking and carousing. She would likely become nervous and lose her advantage. "And some," she continued, "stand about in the store and speak of the adventure they missed because they did not keep close to their brave captain."

The captain's voice went low and growly. "What the blazes are you talking about?"

"Josef Unruh?" She tossed out the name, her voice rising into the question mark. She said not another word, rather allowing its full weight of accusation to come down in the room like a judge's gavel. "What did you do, Dominus? Decide to take the war in Europe into your own hands? Deliver the free world from the dangers of an old man?"

"Unruh? I would not call that brief run-in an adventure." In the ensuing pause, a heavy silence swirled into the captain's study. My father had immediately fallen to the defense of himself for some deed Mother had learned about while in Fairhope yesterday. I could only wonder in prickly fear what my father had done.

"No. You are exactly right. It is an outrage, Dominus. Can it even be true what was told? Can your pride have fallen so low that you assault a crippled man?"

"Unruh's not a cripple. He walks with a limp. So did my father, who could hoist a mainsail to the top of a mast faster than three able-bodied sailors half his age."

"Dominus MacNee, you and your merry men hoisted Josef to the top of a windmill! A man is not sailcloth. And you tied him there and left him alone! Did you think he'd while away time composing free verse in his head? Suppose he had died!"

"Then, my dear, we would have one less German spy in our midst. Whose side are you on? There is a war going on."

"Spy? A German spy? This country is not at war, and if it were, you are not a soldier of its army!"

"Shut up, Lillian!" I dropped Elberta and hurried back down the hall to the study and stood at the door. I cringed when I saw the captain slam his fist down onto the desktop. He raked his open hand quickly sideways, scattering the papers on it to the floor. His pipe went spinning across the room.

Elberta had followed me and stood beside me there in the doorway and also looked into the study, her head lowered in a guarding posture, and yelped. The little mutt

even attempted a growl, which quickly devolved into another broken yelp. The captain took no notice.

"I will remind you, woman, that this is my home and
this is my country and I will not defend myself to you.
Everyone knows that Unruh is a spy! That windmill behind his house is a radio tower. He is sending secret mes-
sages to U-boats in the bay, and with his help America will
be half beaten before we join the war. The only hope of
the world in face of the German dogs lies with us. One
way or the other I will stop Unruh!"

"Oh, my God, Dominus, you have finally succumbed
to the demon rum, its poison sediments have lodged in
your brain. I have never heard a more preposterous . . ."

The captain banged the desk again. The dog whined
and dropped onto its belly at my feet, its muzzle between
its paws. When my father shifted his eyes away from his
wife to glare at me, I expected to be ordered out of the
room. Instead, my father slowly stood and put both palms
down flat on his desk and leaned forward, bringing his
face above the light from the lamp so that his features
caused smoky shadows to rise upward there on his face.
The effect was ghostly. Dominus MacNee's voice was as
even as a prayer, its volume low. "I will remind you"—and
he let his gaze travel from me to my mother, so that it was
clear that he addressed us both—"that I make no effort to
conceal my contempt for the old German. If the chief of
police takes issue with my message to *Herr* Unruh, let him
come knocking on my door."

The captain raised a thick finger, pointing it upward in a professorial gesture, and said, lowering his voice to a rough whisper, but a voice that commanded the silence of the room as a low rumble from down inside a tiger's chest might freeze all other sounds within hearing, "I would sooner scrape for pennies than let go something that requires fixing when I can fix it. If the old German is smart, he will lack the confidence to go outside his own door."

Dominus MacNee stomped his booted foot and bumped the desk with his thigh so that his big brass cup, an ale tankard nine inches tall—holding pencils and a letter opener and a set of dividers and a silver straightedge and a long osprey feather—leaped into the air and fell on its side and off the desktop and thudded to the floor. My mother flinched, and the dog at my feet jumped up and trotted off down the hall toward the front door even though the rain outside fell harder and the wind whooshed through cracks in boards and windowsills and doorjambs.

The captain spun around and marched to a small blackboard standing on an easel near the bookshelves along the wall to the left, snatched up a piece of white chalk from the wooden tray, and wrote in a smooth and elegant hand, *and everywhere the ceremony of innocence is drowned—W. B. Yeats.*

"A line appropriate to the moment from the Irish bard your dear sick mother so loves," my father said. Then he flung the chalk toward his desk and it struck there and broke into two pieces, which rolled onto the floor. I stood away from the door, silent and immobile as the day on the Big Pier when I watched Blue's barrel roll away. The captain slowly walked out of his study and down the hall and outside into the weather without shutting the door, and I could not believe that Elberta followed him, her stumpy tail wagging.

The Irishman known as Blue was a thick-necked man and got his nickname because of his raven's-wing hair and sky-blue eyes, so unlike the ruddy, red-haired, and freckled ethnic stereotype. It was a chilly day two weeks ago when I saw Blue drop his portage onto the dock and lose his balance attempting to avoid a toy truck set rolling in his direction by the Miller twins, the little hellions whose father owned Fairhope Drayage Company. They laughed into their fingers as Blue jumped and sidestepped at the same time, losing his balance and his grip on the small oaken barrel he'd just fetched off the deck of the *Bay Queen*.

There was a heavy crash to the heart pine four-bys beneath Blue's feet. But the barrel's curved staves did not break nor slip the metal band running round them. Instead, the barrel rolled down the dock while Blue danced to regain his balance. And the sound the barrel made as it rolled was like thunder. The scene as it played out invoked in me the same prickly tension I felt when storms grew dark and high in the western sky across the bay, like an army assembling for the onslaught.

That day on the dock I'd been walking behind Blue, a few steps back, when he dropped the barrel, and I had frozen, entranced and intrigued by the sight and the sound of the hogshead rolling toward the handrail at the edge of the Big Pier.

It was odd to find myself so immobilized.

I found that I couldn't dash around Blue to put a hand on the runaway barrel. I could only lean back against the rail and grip it in both hands on either side of my hips and watch the small drama, which was quickly resolved when the barrel rolled into a handrail and came to a stop. Blue yelled at the Miller boys, who poked out their tongues at him and took off running down the dock.

What sorcerer's spell had fixed me to that spot on the rail? It was almost as though a rope had been coiled down from heaven and wound round my arms and legs, forbidding me to move, and in that stillness bade me look closely and see something about myself. But if it was a mirror into which I should look, I saw only a fogged-over fun-house image of someone whose knees were shaky, and I didn't like what I saw.

My father's eyes were amber brown like honey-varnished oak. He was a ship's commander, yes, but had he followed that other calling I had heard him speak of, had he become a professor in a college, he would have commanded a classroom with ease. And his students would have learned well from him, for he was an attentive student in his own studies and displayed his erudition with ease. And, he would have handled dissension in his classroom with authority. If he drew his thatch of black eyebrows together, cutting a furrowing scar between them, those remarkable and piercing eyes smoldered and could stop a man's words, make them drop from the air like cinders from a windblown fire.

I saw it happen that a mere look from Dominus MacNee could silence a man. It was on a Sunday after church when my mother invited Josef Unruh to Magnolia Bayhouse for an afternoon's visit over tea and conversation. This was before the war, before Mr. Unruh became a "German spy," and his first visit to our home—I was maybe thirteen—but it was the first of several other Sunday visits.

Everyone at church knew the man. Mr. Unruh sang in the choir at Saint James', and sometimes sang solo, his deep voice, so rich and full, filling the sanctuary. I saw some close their eyes while he sang. My mother among them.

My mother said, when she told my father in the car one Sunday that she thought she might invite Mr. Unruh over after church someday, that she had "made his acquaintance quite casually" while selecting some short boards at McKean's Hardware with which to build a birdhouse for her mother. Granny Wooten had said she missed her bluebirds that came every year to the tiny house Otis had built for her.

"Why, if I had a plank and a saw, I'd just cobble one together myself," Granny Wooten had said. Mother said with an "ooh" and a clap of her hands that they would do the project together, that it would be a delightful experience. Josef Unruh was in the hardware store and kindly helped my mother pick out her boards.

"Did you know," she asked my father, "that cypress is 30 percent lighter than pine?"

"And not 22 percent?" the captain had laughed, teasing his wife, who—and this surprised me not less than if she'd belched—snapped at my father, and told him that Josef said it, and he knew about wood. I saw a flicker of something in the captain's eyes, but he blinked and looked away, then got up and walked off the porch and into the kitchen.

On his very first visit Mr. Unruh did a strange thing. Josef Unruh, whom I had spoken to only a few times at church, right there on our front porch, quite out of the blue as though he'd been struck with a remarkable idea, offered to give to me an old sloop, a small boat of twenty-five feet. He fairly tumbled into his proposition.

"She is moored in Fly Creek, leaking at ze seams, ja, but stout in her keel and ribs and planking." As Mr. Unruh became increasingly more animated in the description of his sloop, my father's face set harder into a frown.

"You vill perhaps encounter soft wood in ze stem at ze bowsprit, but you vill find ze standing and running rigging are good, ja. Ze sails are yellow but not blown out and she is yours if you'll take her and promise to bring her about shipshape and Bristol fashion. If you need help, I vill lend a hand, now and again."

Josef Unruh was a tall man, over six feet, and with thick forearms and thighs and a neck a little too broad for the rest of his thin frame, which gave a clue to his strength. Even with a limp in his walk, his upright bearing and his shiny black eyes and craggy face would make a man in an alley give way and cut him a wider path than some other man his age. But when he had finished his happy description of the sailboat, and Mr. Unruh turned his face and met my father's eyes, he blinked and swallowed, his surprise nearly palpable. His smile and any more words fell. After a full five-second pause, he added, "That is, of course, if the captain, your father, approves of my offer. . . ."

But Josef Unruh had already reached the point of fracture, and there was no redacting that moment's hard mark on the page of time. Captain Dominus MacNee would not sit for a man, a virtual stranger no less, presuming to have such great familiarity with his son. Other men might look away, and many would, but the captain had been insulted. Back then, to me, it was indiscernible, the rule of conduct that had been breached. But that something had been broken between the two men I did not mistake. My father's eyes never misspoke even the farthest corners of his mind.

And, the captain and Mr. Unruh, it seemed to me, had been abiding well each other's company until the sailboat was brought up. Their talk had been all over the boards. Granny Wooten, as was her wont, helped the subject of poetry onto the gallery, and my father and Mr. Unruh had sparred over the symbolic intent of a poet or two, in this or that quatrain.

I do believe our visitor was surprised to find the ship's captain a literary man. My mother, whom I had never heard discuss literature, derided the topic by saying she'd leave the *men* to discuss *poems*. She took my brother Julian by the hand and walked in the sunshine out onto the dock in front of the house. Granny Wooten happily mediated the whole of the poetry debate.

My mother would have thought it manlier, I assume, when Father and Mr. Unruh began to argue. But I sat on a nearby chair and drank in this conversation that was so like my own poem-centered repartees with Granny Wooten. Jaws became set over Yeats's point of reference for the last part of his poem "The Second Coming," and especially the last two lines: "and what rough beast, its hour come round at last, slouches toward Bethlehem to be born." My father was certain Yeats was making a prediction of world disorder on the scale of biblical prophecies in the New Testament book of Revelation.

Mr. Unruh said my father was wrong, and said just that, *But, Captain, you are wrong,* and therein might have even laid the predicate for the rift that would soon follow. "Yeats was speaking of ze promise," Mr. Unruh said, "of ze domination of man's animal nature as his intellect, ironically, came to overrule his fear of a judgmental God. Do you not agree, sir?"

But there was no give-and-take, and each man dug in. Neither man for the other's point of view gave any quarter. Granny Wooten broke the tension with an offer of tea and biscuits all around and a sly shifting of the topic. The weather is always easy to talk about, especially for a seaman.

"I am so thankful the hurricane season is by, and we were spared this year," she said. Though neither man added a word to her comment, the tension drained away into silence. But then Mr. Unruh made his abrupt offer to give me a sailboat. He might as well have poured a drink on my father, and yet the whole of the captain's rage was conveyed in a silent glare and the knot in his jaw as he clamped down hard on the pipe in his teeth.

And I did not mistake his anger, though at the time I was uncertain of its motivation. At whatever risk, however, I was a boy not willing to forfeit a sailboat. I asked the captain if I could keep the boat. Since my father had not actually spoken aloud any objection, to forbid my request would have dragged onto the porch something as yet too ill formed for my father to articulate. And so the captain answered, perhaps too quickly, that it mattered not a whit to him.

Within minutes the German stood and brushed away from his khaki pants some imaginary crumbs. He excused himself to leave, and as he was walking away, he made a big detour across the yard. I believe this was another, and worse, affront to my father when he called out, "Excuse me, Mrs. MacNee," attracting the attention of my mother.

"Thank you for your company," he shouted to her as she and Julian stopped their stroll and Mother waved to Mr. Unruh. "It has been my pleasure," he added, then he turned and disappeared through the hedges at the far side of the yard.

When Mr. Unruh had left that day, I continued to wonder about what had transpired between my father and him. It did not seem to me likely that arguing literary criticism had been enough to spark the captain's infamous glare. But here he was behaving as though a stranger had placed his innocent son's hand into the pale palm of one of his Creole whores. A blind man could see on my father's face the workings of the subterranean disturbance this German had birthed.

I sat near the window in my bedroom and the glass panes were dusty and hazed, old and wavy and freckled with tiny bubbles here and there. On the outside they were powdered with the evaporated residue from years of brackish mist swirling up from the whitecaps running before hard winds and full gales. The blows ripped in at a westerly slant across Mobile Bay, strong from the south, but stronger from the north. I sat in a small Windsor chair with fine delicate spindles of light maple arranged in a comfortable arc across my back.

I had found the chair washed up on the beach, half buried in the sand after a late-season hurricane last fall. I salvaged the chair and enjoyed moments of romantic speculation about whose pier or dock or porch had lost the chair, whether it was from across the bay in Bayou La Batre or Belle Fontaine, or down south, maybe all the way from Fort Morgan. I kept the fantasy going all through my repairs to the chair—reseating three of seven spindles into the steam-bent bow of the back, and replacing a lateral rung between the legs—and then the sanding and varnishing.

I did the work in my father's woodshop, a cottage-sized clay-block building several yards off to the side of Magnolia Bayhouse and down a path between overgrown azaleas. The shop was a favorite place of mine, cozy and inviting with a cedar shake roof and blocks of reddish-orange clay dug from the banks of Fish River down east of town and fired there at a kiln operation called Clay City Brick Works.

The small building had large windows for good light and cooling breezes in the summer, a cast-iron potbelly stove to warm the space in the winter, and a tongue-and-groove pine-plank floor that was easy on the feet and legs when standing for long periods. I do believe my best moments with my father were there, when the captain would invite me down to the woodshop to help with some small project. Father's voice had never been calmer or more pleasant than when he explained the use of a tool, the right technique for planing or joining two pieces of wood, how to use the glue and clamps. At times, he'd puff on his pipe and watch me in silence.

My father handled his tools with a deft grace, his fingers relaxed and like a priest's turning Bible pages on the pulpit.

"See, if you turn over this flat rasp, son, the back side of it is convex with bigger teeth." He rubbed the barbs with his thumb.

"And if you give a gentle roll with your wrist as you push the rasp across the wood, not too much pressure, mind you, then you transfer that motion into a curvature in the piece you are working."

All these many years and I still have the two hand-shaped snow geese in flight hanging on the wall back of my desk. Their wings of hammered copper are tacked to polished dark walnut.

I made one of the snow geese.

My father made the other.

We worked on them side by side, and when we had finished, my father said he was pleased with my work. This, his purest blessing, gave me flight that day and holds me aloft even now.

Then, almost suddenly, work in the woodshop stopped and my father began to smell more and more often of whiskey. He began to stay away from home for longer periods of time. Still, I would go to the shop and sometimes I would sit for a long minute, just looking around at my father's tools. And then I'd commence my work alone, but the woodshop was so much my father's that I could almost feel him there beside me.

And I missed him.

In that space, where we had communed, there with his oiled blades and saws, as close there as a father and son can be, I missed him. At other places around Magnolia Bayhouse, I was relieved and glad he was absent. More, was sometimes stirred to hate his recent history on the premises. But in the woodshop, I wanted him beside me.

My skill with woodworking grew, and the time I spent alone had the effect of transforming hours into minutes, for me a kind of unclocking of time. I knew that my scarcity of friends grew out of this comfort in solitude, my contentment at being alone on a dock on the bay with my cast net. Those days or afternoons when I was not at school I whiled away in the shop with the myriad saws and knives and the smell of pine and oak, of cypress and cedar shavings curling onto the floor as the sweet aroma filled the room.

In the woodshop I had spent maybe six, seven hours on the Windsor chair and now it was my favorite place to sit and read and I kept it situated near the tall window facing the bay at the front of my bedroom.

When I sat in my bedroom and read I enjoyed the abundant natural light that fell from the high sash onto the page of my open book. At night there was a small lamp and table nearby, and I kept whatever book, or books, I was currently reading on that table.

On this Saturday morning, drawing nigh to noon, I sat there by the window in the good light and reached over to the lamp table and took a book into my lap. I looked out the window while absentmindedly flipping through the pages of my dog-eared copy of *Huckleberry Finn*. I stopped turning the pages and looked down at the open book, not really reading. I'd already read *Huck Finn* three times through. Today I just mostly sat with my thoughts as they glided over the top of my mind like so many pelicans skimming over their liquid reflections. Granny Wooten had died two days ago in the afternoon on Thanksgiving Day.

They had come that day for her body when the rain stopped and taken it and prepared it for burial, and it now lay in state in the parlor at Magnolia Bayhouse. I resumed scanning my book, lost and scattered in my thinking.

Occasionally I stopped and read a favorite passage, some of those lines or paragraphs that I and Granny Wooten had traded back and forth and discussed or read to each other so many times.

In chapter 6, my eyes fell upon a paragraph that began, "He kept me with him all the time, and I never got a chance to run off." I was there and then struck with a thought, something Granny had said: "Huck ran away. Some boys, you know, do just that. Up and run away."

And in recalling her words I had quite a reckoning: Granny Wooten's gift of Mark Twain's Mississippi River tale bore her tacit permission for me to leave the captain and my mother. I could run away.

I left my seat to go to my grandmother's gunmetal gray casket. I thought I might give her a conspiratorial nod and a wink to acknowledge our little secret. Perhaps I could glean from her some will to actually leave this house for good. Huck had cut and run. There was the model. But I needed the gumption. Granny Wooten would have had the gumption and the gall to do the deed. Indeed, Granny Wooten had made her escape, though her body was still here snug in its last bed on this earth in the front parlor pushed up beside the hearth.

I walked slowly into the room but for some reason could not look into the open casket. Above the casket was a four-inch-thick rough-sawn cedar mantelboard set with vases of perfumey flowers and sympathy cards and an oddment of family photographs. People, some I did not even know, looked out at me from dusty frames of polished mahogany and at least one of silver, and one, a five-by-seven, was carved ivory. My eyes continued to resist my grandmother's corpse and played instead along the mantelpiece and the assorted pictures in their frames.

In the ivory frame was a picture of Dominus MacNee and Lillian Wooten. They leaned there shoulder to shoulder, the captain's arm around his pretty girl's waist drawing her close as they reposed, smiling. Always smile for the camera. But, for the truth of it, I wouldn't mind one picture with anger, or sadness. Just for reference, you know.

Any scrapping between my parents had been just as out of sight as their intimacies until, like the captain's Scotch whisky, everything got put on the table in plain view. Granny Wooten had once told me after breakfast as I helped her clean up in the kitchen (and neither Mother nor Father had joined the meal), "It's a coward who'll pour out his anger on innocent bystanders. And cowards are the most dangerous animals on the planet." And I believed she must have feared some uncertain outcome between the captain and me or she would not have thought I should run away.

I stood there still thinking about what she'd said as my

mother walked through the kitchen and out the door. I moved to the window and watched her go down on the beach and sit down on a driftwood log. Her neck was straight and her shoulders squared. I could divine the anger she cast in the direction of the waves. Then I had heard the captain's truck fire up and drive away.

"Your father," Granny Wooten said, "is not the only one who can just up and leave, boy." Not until this day had I put it all together that it was I who could just up and leave.

I stepped up beside the open casket. Even in death's repose on the tufted white satin, the resemblance between my grandmother and my mother was plain to see. I wondered if the two were somehow in league with one another on the idea of my leaving. Sometimes I could almost make it out, like an image across the meadow's morning fog that might be a deer or it might be a cow, I could almost apprehend that something in my father's disdain for me was possibly traceable to his disdain for his wife.

It was a feeling that was probably born of a keen awareness of Mother's doting preference for me over Julian. And there was a dim sense that even I got more attention from her than did Father.

Now and again when the captain bristled and stomped about and tilted up his Scotch whisky bottle, I would catch him looking at me not with eyes like those he employed to rattle an opponent, but with eyes that bore such malice that I felt a cold tingling in the pit of my stomach. And it was then that I grew to hate liquor, appropriating to the oily juice the meanness that issued from my father. The stuff vilely exaggerated the captain's emotions.

And I blamed the whiskey for taking from me moments like those shared in the woodshop, for driving them off like the precious minutes were no more than a flock of pestering crows.

But my father was sober as Granny Wooten when his anger was fanned to flame over the gift of the sloop. I suppose I could have justified that it was the boat of Josef Unruh itself that day that proved to be the plank in my father's eye, that I should then, as a good son, renounce the boat. Cast away the offending member. On the other hand, it was a boat, and not a boy's boat. It was a man's boat and it could go places where a man would want to go and it was now my boat and I would not give it up. I would not part with it on the off chance that this might buy for me a smile from my father.

Before I stepped away from my grandmother's casket, I actually moved closer, close enough to have reached inside to rest my fingers atop hers. I considered the warmth I had known from her hands, her palms against my cheeks when I would come in from the beach red-faced, my hair damp from the wind across the wavetops. *Just like your Grandfather Otis, so alive when you're near the water.* I could almost hear her.

Her voice seemed nearer to me than my own breathing and I almost took Granny Wooten's hand, but the rings on her fingers I had never seen. I knew they must be some keepsake of hers, brought out for this occasion of her burial. But I knew, too, that she had not herself put on the rings and that someone had lifted her unresisting fingers and adorned them without permission, and that seemed to me such complete proof that she was dead that I closed my eyes and stepped away. I turned and left the room.

I wished for the wake to be over, for the people

to all go home, for the food to be carried away. Mrs. Wilson, one of the teachers from Organic School, had eaten two chicken legs without leaving the table and without stopping her story about the German U-boat she and her husband could swear they had seen surface in Mobile Bay.

"The Kaiser's men," Mrs. Wilson misspoke, "will not leave us out of this. They covet our amber waves of grain." Kate Smith would have been pleased, I thought. I knew the water's depth in Mobile Bay, and did not believe a submarine could travel beneath its waves. On the other hand, nor would I have believed that one woman would eat two chicken legs in such quick succession. But funerals are a field day for big appetites.

I'm not sure what appetite I was satisfying when I walked into the kitchen and risked grown-up familiarity with one of my father's men, Percy Mead, saying "So, Mr. Mead, it's told the German was taught a lesson. That's so, I reckon."

The man was enough the braggart to respond with a grin. "Thing was, he didn't put up much of a fuss. Odd-like. After we'd got hold of him good, he just kind of locked his lips and bunched his arms, but never said a word. We fixed a stout halter on him and hoisted him up to the top of that windmill. Four of us hauled on the line—he's kind of a big man, you know—but the captain cleated him off up there and gave him a warning. I never learned who let him down. Did you hear?"

"No, sir. I didn't hear." I choked down my anger and embarrassment, and excused myself and walked away wondering how the man I knew as a good carpenter and boatwright had incited such hatred.

Not soon enough, my grandmother's body would be taken in its hinged metal box to the graveyard at the church, and this party would be over.

My mother would swallow her sadness, remembering how she had accomplished that feat four years earlier when Grandpa Otis had passed away. And, in the same way, all over again, her inability to contain all her emotions would cause her to break down at odd moments during an ordinary act on an ordinary day. I would, again, as then, look away and let her have those moments. They were hers to have. My own grief was lodged in my chest where no one could see it, and that is where I would keep it.

I spoke a quiet good-bye to Granny Wooten and made my way down the short hall toward my room. I would not mix with the company spread throughout the rest of the house, did not wish to make small talk. I didn't know where my mother or father had got off to, and I had not seen them since early morning. My chair and window and book would keep me well enough until time to go to the church. I knew no one would come to my room. I could wait in privacy there, even watch through the window the people wandering about the grounds. So I was surprised to find someone sitting in my chair when I entered the small bedroom.

"I hope you don't mind, Rove," said Anna Pearl Anderson. She closed my copy of *Huckleberry Finn* and placed her hands over it, pressing down the loose folds of her dress there in her lap. She smiled, but seemed to take it back, as though remembering the occasion.

"If you like," she said, "I'll leave. It's just that my mother is being the good schoolmarm and greeting everyone here with the earnestness of a politician and I cannot think what to do with my face when people look at me." The girl set the book back on the lamp table and was about to rise when I finally spoke to her.

"No, please," I said, "you're welcome to hide out in here. That's what I'm doing just now. It's a good spot for laying low."

She sat back down and looked intently at me. Anna Pearl was probably two years older, and her mother was the headmistress at my school, the Marietta Johnson School of Organic Education, and I could not fathom why she'd come into my room. Who would go uninvited into the bedroom of anyone but a dear and close friend?

Only my brother and mother and father had ever been into this room since it had become mine. I had not turned two, I'd been told, when the captain's father died. Magnolia Bayhouse became the property of my father, and he and Mother had moved into the master bedroom, leaving me this room. Julian got the other bedroom. There was a guest room. My claim to the front bedroom with its bay view windows had never even been tested.

More, it was no one's business, I felt, and was guilty of wearing that conviction on my chest, that I retreated behind this door as a matter of course, and I stared at the floor and wondered why in God's name I'd told Anna Pearl that I hid out in here.

"You look nice," she said, appraising me from my shiny black shoes and creased dark trousers to my top-buttoned white shirt. "I don't think I've ever seen you with your hair combed so neatly." And with that Anna Pearl did smile, and I was sure it was because my face was warming red.

"Granny Wooten," I blurted out, "liked for me to comb my hair. She said she was afraid I'd attract seabirds to my nest if I didn't keep out the tangles."

"Well, she would be mighty proud of your natty appearance today. And all just for her. She'd be honored, Rove. It's sweet of you."

I was flustered. Anna Pearl Anderson was the prettiest girl on the Eastern Shore, I believed, and had I had a sense of a world broader than that bayfront crescent of thirty-five miles—Spanish Fort to the north, through Fairhope and south to Great Point Clear, or maybe a little farther down the bay to Mullet Point—I would have easily included all such known territories in my appraisal of her comparative beauty.

She was almost as tall as I and had a nimble gait that suggested her full-spirited manner and a certain restlessness. Her auburn hair was full and wavy and always caught the sun in a way like the swells on Mobile Bay in August. And her eyes, no one could prepare you for her eyes. The green of them was between jade and the shadowy bright leaves on a springtime dogwood tree. One glance from her promised you'd never have the upper hand, assured you the unexpected.

Plus, it was alluring to me that she was seventeen, close to eighteen.

I'd noticed her at school. I found it provocative, of course, when she'd strike that hip-out-to-the-side completely girlish pose, but it was also provocative when I later learned that she could pinpoint the little mistakes I sometimes made when my net fell into the water a crumpled mess. More, she was able to demonstrate how to correct the toss. She could make a sweet cast that any old-timer would be proud of. Her self-assurance, as we became better friends, at times turned a little bossy: "A diary! Rove MacNee, don't you know that is a girly thing for a boy to do? For heaven's sake, at least follow in the seafaring tradition of men like your father and call your scribblings a logbook."

Which suggestion seemed to me, at first, as goofy as my diary seemed to her effeminate. But then as I, and later she in league with me, continued the secret overhaul work on the *Sea Bird* tied bow and stern to sycamores in Fly Creek, the notion of keeping a logbook, not a diary, came to appeal to me. The subtle shift could even lift me a few degrees above my lubberliness, though I was not a green clodbuster by any means. After all, I'd sailed and worked the deck three whole summers on the *Mary Foster*. But seafaring confidence gained by any means, including my little fantasies about keeping a logbook, would all be necessary should I actually cast off and sail away.

We both gave a start when someone just outside the window, standing on the gallery, screamed so loud it seemed to ring off the walls in my bedroom and gain strength and volume on the back-bounce. I almost fell to the window in my trouble to see what was going on. Anna Pearl leapt out of my path, up from the little chair, knocking it over backward.

There was such a scurrying of people on the porch and in the yard that I could make no sense of it. I heard only scraps of words and phrases through the closed window, but "gunshot" was a word I heard a second and third time. I turned and bounded for the bedroom door. Anna Pearl was right behind me as we made for the front door, brushing into, or knocking past, a confusion of people as we went.

"What in God's name?" was the first thing I heard out on the porch, and that from Father Harvey Jones. Several, as they careered about the yard, were pointing out toward the bay. Then I saw what the others were gesturing toward: my father. Captain Dominus MacNee stood amidships of his flat-bottomed skiff, wide-legged like a freebooter of old in defiant stance, as the boat drifted a scant twenty yards offshore. He bore a rifle held at something like parade arms, but his finger in the trigger guard would have drawn the attention of even a weak eye. Such is the capacity of the human brain and its helpmates to discern danger.

Anna Pearl stood behind me and placed both hands on my shoulders, leaning out and looking past me toward the wild-haired buccaneer threatening the crowd of mourners at Granny Wooten's wake.

"Rove, why, that's your father!" Anna Pearl dropped her hands and moved to stand beside me, then caught my forearm with a strong grip.

"Yes." More a croak from me than an actual word.

"What is he doing?"

"Well, he fired his damn rifle at his own home!" A man standing nearby, someone I did not recognize, spoke angrily with a British accent, but did not look the least bit flustered. "Or, more precisely, the tree branches above his home. See there—" and he pointed to a crooked arm-thick limb, five feet long, from a much longer branch that dipped toward the eave of the house beside the porch. The limb was scraggly with Spanish moss, and its end was a bundle of exploded yellow wood splinters poking out of a gray bark sleeve.

The captain's skiff had drifted down the bay a bit and nearer the beach. The little dog Elberta came dashing onto the sand there and dropped her muzzle between her paws and barked with such energy that her body bounced with each *woof, woof.*

My father took no notice of the mutt and shifted the rifle to his left hand, and bent and took up a long oar and poled the boat one-armed until he was back in front of Magnolia Bayhouse. As he tossed the oar into the bottom of his skiff and resumed a ready posture, the rifle held like one leg of an X across his chest, Dominus MacNee began yelling.

"Lillian, send the German outside and give me a clean shot at the bastard." The captain's voice cut like a cannonball through the air toward the crowd, and there was a murmur from the people still anxiously milling about. Several had run to the back of the house and others had scampered inside; some automobiles had cranked up and were leaving.

Julian suddenly appeared at my side and I spun him around in the middle of his query, "What is Father . . . ?"

"Julian, get back inside. Now! Please go find Mother." The urgency in my tone carried enough authority to get him moving.

But no sooner had Julian departed than I was surprised and disquieted to see Josef Unruh step onto the gallery. I'd seen him earlier, minutes after my exchange with Mr. Percy. The German had come inside, not mixing with others, but seeking out and expressing his condolences to Mother. I had looked about for Father when the tall man walked into the house and removed his hat. His presence was an outright invitation to disaster. And calamity was tightening its noose like the coiling of a fat water moccasin.

Fear and anger flickered through the crowd in the yard.

The man at my side said, "The chap's gone crazy. Someone's got to do something before some innocent bloke is shot."

I said calmly, "My father will hit only the target he's aiming at. Mr. Unruh should step inside."

"Rove, what are you saying?" Anna Pearl was becoming frantic, snatching on my sleeve.

The British fellow whirled to face me. "Hello, what, indeed, are you saying there? And who the blazes is Mr. Unruh?"

But I had nothing more to say and turned in a hurry and was headed to warn Josef Unruh that he should find his way quickly to the back door of Magnolia Bayhouse. I felt no obligation to protect Mr. Unruh in any way; this idea to prevent a face-to-face confrontation was for my father. I had to make some effort to keep him from the consequences of his MacGregor-inherited temper. I had to try to get Mr. Unruh out of our house, off our property, and went to find him.

Anna Pearl's mother rushed past me, catching her daughter two steps behind me, crying out, "Anna Pearl, we must leave at once!"

Another shot was fired and I jerked around to see Father squeeze off another round straight up into the air as the bow of his skiff beached on the sand. Looking back, I saw that Josef Unruh had stepped out of Magnolia Bayhouse and was standing on the porch.

If I thought my father might be drunk, the notion was dispelled with the agility and grace with which he carefully placed his rifle athwart the skiff, its barrel resting in the oarlock, and sprang over the gunwale and hit the sand at a gallop, chasing up a small dune growing around the tangle of roots at the base of a giant longleaf pine.

Elberta nipped frantically at my father's heels. He took no notice and barreled past a tree that looked about to fall. The tree's pronounced westerly lean, from fighting waves and tidal erosion, and gales and hurricanes, might have been pointing the way across the open water and out of this foolishness.

A banshee-like wail issued from Father's wide-open mouth as he ran, and Elberta headed for cover. In another deft movement, while bounding full-tilt, the captain bent slightly and his swinging arm came up with a curving broad-bladed knife. It had been sheathed in a leather scabbard buckled just above his boot top.

Now, almost unbidden, like a thought of a pretty girl during the prayer at supper, it came to me that if men could be separated from their passions by a physical distance, say a turning, tumbling river, nice and wide and deep like the old Mississippi, if men could only stand and shake their fists across a mile or so of turbulent silted water, if their voices were lost to the thunderous moan rising up from the bottom of the Mississippi River bed, it just might keep some men out of jail and other men alive.

But there was no river to cage back the temper of Dominus MacNee. In fact, there was nothing, and no one, no heroes, it seemed, to fall on the bomb rolling into this morning. There were only gaping spectators to this sport of madness and misguided patriotism. I wondered, did my father really believe in a threat of espionage, that Josef Unruh was in league with Hitler's U-boat commanders, that his windmill on a hilltop was providing information critical to Germany's war with the world?

The answer, I believed, would come out in the courtroom. That's where this fracas was likely headed. Maybe if I could prevent my father from reaching Josef Unruh, it would not be a murder trial.

My stomach twisted. My father was running, the knife held cupped in his hand, almost concealing it, the blade tucked close to his wrist. Josef Unruh was standing, crouched in a defensive gesture, at the top of the steps leading onto the gallery. Neither man was going to give way, and the growl coming from my father incited further panic among the bystanders.

People ran this way and that. One fat woman overdressed with a fine heavy winter coat fell backward over a gnarled root of the big magnolia tree near the corner of the house. She squealed and cried *hooo, hooo,* long and drawn out, and some thought she had become a victim in the melee.

But no one rushed to her aid, as the principal drama was unfolding in the other direction. Most bystanders kept graveyard still and breathed shallow as if such would maybe make this all go away. Their behavior was appropriate to a surprise encounter with a rattlesnake: If one will just be calm and move easy or not at all, there is some good chance the viper will go on its merry way. The captain's strike, however, was not to be avoided.

Before I could interfere in some way, at least, it was too late. Josef Unruh leaped from the porch, landing on his assailant, and they rolled on the ground together as screams and pandemonium rose higher into the treetop canopy over Magnolia Bayhouse.

I thought of the chief of police, Owen Carter, and heard above the din someone else call Chief Carter's name, but I didn't see him and did not believe he had come to the wake today. He had come by yesterday to express his sympathy and had stayed quite a long time talking to Father on the gallery. It was too late for someone to fetch him to this scene.

I raced up to the men, grunting, tangled together on the dirt in front of the porch. Both men's faces were covered with dirt, and the captain's shirt was ripped open at the buttons. I was only superficially aware of the nearby crowd of kin and friends and neighbors who'd known Granny Wooten. If I'd been inclined to worry for the old German, he had no need of it. Josef Unruh had taken control of the captain's knife arm and managed to get the higher position and had his knee on the forearm of the captain.

Just as the older man reached to wrest the knife away from the hand that posed the lethal threat, Dominus MacNee came up with his own knee into the side of the man atop him, making full contact with his rib cage and knocking the wind from Josef Unruh. Watching Father lurch from underneath Mr. Unruh, I felt that old tightening in my belly because he knew this advantage would not be wasted. I dreaded what was coming.

The six-inch curved blade in Father's hand, the knife that he'd honed to a razor-sharp edge, was going to be what brought this fight to its terrible conclusion.

Not one among the watchers stepped forward. I could only watch my father raise the knife and could only scream, "Father, please! Just stop it! Mister Unruh!"

And at the calling of his name, just at that moment, as if answering some malicious teacher's roll call, Josef Unruh, the big man, was sliced across the back, crosswise from his shoulder down to his wide and smooth black leather belt.

"Oh, God," I said.

A woman howled, and the baby in her arms set to squalling. There was a flood of deep crimson. In no time the blood soaked the fringes of the new vent made there in the cotton fabric of Josef Unruh's shirt by the swish of that butcher-sharp stainless steel in the captain's right hand.

"Aaaah!" came from the wounded man, more like a painful sigh, full of defeat as he rolled over on the grass and away from the captain. "Dominus MacNee, you son of a bitch."

"No. You, sir, will learn that traitors to this country are offered no mercy," the captain growled. Now that he was up on one knee, huffing deep breaths, like a winded bull, the captain's neck and arms and chest were shining with sweat. "And the worst of it is I've only nicked you."

My father's brown eyes danced. The way he stood there over the downed man and calmly plowed his fingers through his wavy, uncombed hair, shining raven black with gray streaks like Father Brown's, one might have thought he was getting ready to step onto a dance floor and ask one of his Creole ladies to dance. He did not act like a man who'd just knifed someone.

I watched Josef Unruh pull himself into a curl like a shrimp dropped from a morning's toss of my net. Mr. Unruh was groaning, growing pale.

No sooner did Dominus MacNee wipe a red stain onto his pants leg from the blade of his knife than three women rushed up to the man on the ground, hissing at the captain to back off. The women immediately set to tending Josef Unruh with clean white towels brought outside from Magnolia Bayhouse. One of them yelled for her husband to bring around their automobile for transporting the patient to the clinic. The women held cloth hard and flat in thick folds against the bloody seam across the fallen man's back.

My father looked around. "Are there others who want to have a go with me? Try to stop me from putting this man out of his traitorous business!" No one spoke or moved.

"You fool, Dominus. What have you done?"

I had given no thought to Mother. I had not taken time to wonder why she was not on hand to witness the

sorry scene in her front yard. Then she was there and immediately ran up to her husband and tried to slap him, but
the captain snatched her hand out of the air and twisted
her arm.

"Just leave Mother alone," I said, "She isn't . . ."

And I was caught across the mouth with a backhand
that whipped my head back and instantly puffed my lips
and filled my mouth with blood, blurring my vision and
setting me off balance. I stumbled backward and bit off
the words in my brain, so near to my tongue.

I only looked at my father, who looked back at me, and
we stared at each other until Anna Pearl stepped up beside
me and told me in a voice easily heard by the captain that
the police chief had arrived. Anna Pearl's mother had
taken my mother aside and was holding her in a manner
she might employ to comfort a child at her school.

"I suppose, Unruh, that you will live until I am released
from the town jail," my father said. "But, you stand ad-
vised to leave this place and never come back. If you fail to
heed my warning, you will discover that I am not through
with you."

The captain held his knife in his fist and stood in a
military posture until Chief Carter's car was forty feet
away and sliding on the gravel. The car was braked too
hard, got a little sideways, and nosed down to a stop with
the bumper not three feet from Mother's prize marble
miniature statue of Saint Francis of Assisi. Monkey grass,
thick and green, crowded its base.

I knew what my father was up to when he held his knife up in the air. He wanted to be certain the policeman saw him when he threw it down, and he finally tossed it, end-overing, almost like slow motion, to land inches away from my feet.

"Take care of my knife, Son, until the High Sheriff has finished having his important moment and brings me back to this driveway in a day or two. Now go down on the beach and tend to my skiff, and bring my rifle inside the house. Do that now."

I did not move to do my father's bidding. I wiped sweat from my forehead with the heel of my palm.

Someone yelled, "Where the Sam Hill have you been, Owen Carter? Five more minutes we might have had another croaker on this place."

Kate Anderson jerked her head around as if she might catch the misbehaving, bad-mannered man who'd spoken so rudely. She let go her hug and gave a last, inquiring look at Lillian MacNee, and stepped to her daughter's side. She took Anna Pearl's arm. "Come along, Anna Pearl. This is no place for you. Say good-bye to Rove. You will see him in school on Monday."

"But, Mother, I thought we were going to the funeral. . . ."

"We have shared our condolences with the family. Now, say good-bye and come along." Anna Pearl did not say anything to me, but turned in a huff and walked away from her mother, her dress swishing.

"Rove, I'm sorry this happened," Anna Pearl's mother said. "Take care of Lillian, and I will see you in school on Monday."

She turned and hurried along a path between two large, overgrown azaleas at the corner of the house to catch up to her daughter. Chief Carter nodded and half-heartedly lifted his left hand as he passed them, his right hand remaining clamped on his revolver.

Though Josef Unruh had not yet been taken away to the doctor, I could hear the low babble resume, heard kids beginning to skitter around in the yard. I noticed some of the elders crab-pinch or shush this and that boy and girl.

The women were tending well to Josef Unruh; my mother now among the nursing brood. Everyone knew by the captain's demeanor that he did not believe he had de-livered to his foe a fatal wound, and so the crowd's behav-ior followed the captain and a lighter mood arose among them. But there was a final scene playing out here on this open-air stage: the arrest of Captain Dominus MacNee. He was handcuffed and put into the police car. And this action was carried out by a friend of the captain's and his family.

I knew how it would go. Chief Owen Carter would ask Father politely to take a seat in his patrol car, and the captain would do as he was asked and would sit in jail, well fed with fresh bedding on his cot, and something to read, for some little stay. Probably three days at most. During that time Granny Wooten would have been buried, and prayed for, and sung into heaven.

And my father, for missing those services at Saint James' Church, would be by many people cursed to hell with enough venom and potent hexing to keep his soul in hock someplace until he died and caught up with it. Then Dominus MacNee, to hear some of the old ones tell it, would burn for eternity.

M*y father was heard* to brag that our forebears in the Old Country had been MacGregors, the bloodiest clan in the Highlands, and that Mac-Nees were honor-bound to keep the code Cousin Rob Roy laid down in the middle of the seventeenth century. It could be argued that many in Fairhope, by other surnames, could claim kin to Rob Roy MacGregor, if feuding was the reddest thread in the bloodline. I knew my father did not hold the copyright on the belief that it was right to use a rifle or his knife to right a wrong, to take an eye for an eye. There were plenty of Fairhopers who would have bragged all the way to the gallows.

And I can say, too, that a mean and drunken father was not a claim to fame in peaceful Fairhope. Dominus MacNee, simply, was just mine to deal with. And I got no comfort that some other boys seemed to have it just as bad. Derrell Flowers had to deal with Bonefish Gilbert, a swamp-slime stepfather who once tied him up and left

him in the woods all night to cure the boy's fear of the
dark. But, my story was pretty much the only one I was
truly concerned with. And is that not the way with most
of us, most of the time? "There but for the grace of God
go I," seems to me a feeble affect toward real empathy. If
such wisdom is uttered when you look at another person
in a wheelchair, for instance, what real connection have
you made to that person's misery while standing there on
your two good legs?

Everyone, I think, has some mean and sorry portion to
deal with. If you have a headache, you might, indeed, tell
someone of your pain, but it is your headache, and yours
only. Captain Dominus MacNee was my own headache.
And if I'm fair about my predicament, old Huck had it
worse than Derrell, or I. At least Bonefish Gilbert and the
good captain had not, so far, tried to kill Derrell or me.

I say that other boys had their fatherly crosses to bear,
but, of course, the girls of my youth had crazy and violent
fathers, too. I simply almost never heard their stories.

Anna Pearl Anderson had no qualms editorializing,
however, about my lot. She showed up at Granny Wooten's
funeral driving the Organic School truck, and I was sure
her mother didn't know she'd taken it. She might as well
have driven the big tires right over my head because she
told me she believed the fight she had just witnessed was
the behavior of a jealous man.

At first, I did not apprehend her meaning.

"What do you think of that?" she asked.

Then, as it developed in my head, what she was suggesting: "What?"

I must have looked at her as though she were a tree full of pelicans, the way she became so defensive.

"Well, I'm saying," she said, with her eyebrows high and her hands on her hips, "that I saw two men fighting like they were settling a barroom feud over a woman. That's what I saw, and I have a really good eye for this sort of thing." That this girl had never seen a barroom feud over a woman was a point lost to the deeper implications of what she had said to me when we were finally walking away from the cemetery.

We had waited there together as flowers were set about the mound of dirt covering the new burial. Then Anna Pearl stayed back when I walked to the graveside. I stood there alone and bowed my head. I closed my eyes, not so much in the reverence of prayer as the wish to call up Granny Wooten's face.

I was at first troubled that only darkness draped itself over my mind, but then I blinked my eyes open and smiled. "I guess you really are gone, Granny." I was sure she felt my little wish that she keep an eye out for me, and I knew that she would.

I rejoined Anna Pearl and we walked away in the silence of the chilly afternoon. We stopped only briefly when my mother and two of her friends, and Julian with one of the other woman's sons, greeted us on the path from the cemetery back to the church. Mother put her hand on my shoulder. The other women and the boys kept on toward the grave.

"We'll miss her," she said, her eyes reddening.

"We will," I said. Anna Pearl waited several steps farther down the path, looking in the other direction. I didn't know what else to say, so I said nothing. Then I told Mother I'd get Anna Pearl to give me a ride home.

"Julian and I will be along soon." She patted my arm and went on down the path to her waiting friends, and to Julian and the other boys already romping and chasing among the gravestones.

Anna Pearl fell into step beside me, and I don't know how far we walked. I had my face down, said nothing. In fact, I was occupied with crazy notions of Granny Wooten, wondering how Magnolia Bayhouse would reconcile her passing. When she had been alive in those rooms, her spirit could be felt in the very walls, the floor. If Granny Wooten wasn't at home when I'd come in from the schoolhouse, I could actually feel the emptiness of the place. I could feel the house waiting for her to come home.

Then Anna Pearl said, "Do you think I'm crazy when I say your father is jealous of Mr. Unruh?" I suppose she hoped her words had by now wound their way through my befuddlement, wobbled around, and got completely through to me. I stopped in my tracks. A cooling breeze had come up, and the playful wind blew strands of hair about her face, but her eyes were unmoving and locked onto mine, as if I should not defy her. Her gaze was so unblinking and she was so lovely that I could only shake my head.

"I'm only saying what I saw," she said.

Something subterranean broke loose in me and an eruption ensued. "Oh, no. I'm delighted that you think my father and Mr. Unruh have some score to settle over my mother. My God, Anna Pearl! Is this your idea of funeral chatter? My grandmother just died and I'm not even out of the cemetery good and you come up with all this."

"Well, your father might really believe Mr. Unruh is a spy or something." She actually tried to smile, and instead she shook her head and cleared her voice with a little nervous cough. She affected a frown to make her face appear serious when she said, "The fact is your father is sitting in jail, maybe for attempted murder, and maybe for a long time, Rove. There is plenty of smoke here, and the fire is over something besides some war across the ocean. I'd bet my shoes on it."

When I am inclined, in afterthought, to say that I still cannot believe Anna Pearl Anderson chose the very hour of my grandmother's funeral to suggest that my mother might be fooling around with a man, I remind myself it was that same morning that my father chose to get himself put into jail for assaulting and battering a man. I am also reminded of the fire-bearing spirit of that girl.

It was Monday, and the captain had been in his cell since Saturday afternoon. I sat in the study at my father's big desk waiting while Mother finished packing a lunch for the prisoner. She had asked me to stay home from school and drive her into town. I sat forward and folded my arms over the leather-cornered blotter in the center of the desk. I was feeling drowsy, had not slept well again last night.

The morning's soft light angled through the window and pooled warmly on the frayed corner of the Oriental rug. The rug, with its faded reds and soft blues, yellows almost gone to white, had been a gift to the captain's father from a Greek visiting the port of Mobile to check on one of his ships. I'd heard my father say he liked the way the sun was robbing the rug of its color, reminding him of his own numbered days, and he'd refused to let my mother move it from its place in front of the tall window.

"Let's go, Rove." Mother's voice startled me.

"I'm sorry. I know this is exhausting. Maybe it'll be over soon."

With something like a clairvoyant's clear sight, I doubted it.

We went outside to the car, and I opened the passenger door for Mother. She sat down and held in her lap the basket with food in it. I shut the heavy door and went to the other side and settled myself at the wheel. The eight-cylinder motor fired right up, and I drove the family sedan, a black Buick four-door, out our driveway and up the bayfront road called Mobile Street. Huge pines and live oaks stood near the road like sentries and shaded our going.

At the intersection at the foot of Fairhope Avenue, I turned right and up the hill into the center of town. Behind me, Fairhope Avenue dropped downhill to the busy waterfront goings-on at the Big Pier. I turned north at the main intersection and parked in front of the police station and jail. Chief Owen Carter was the only peace officer employed by the city, and his black-and-white police car, a 1940 Ford, was in the spot just ahead of where I stopped the Buick.

Chief Owen Carter was very businesslike with my mother and said he would not release his prisoner until Josef Unruh's condition improved, and the man had not made much gain.

"He lost a lot of blood, Miss Lillian," Chief Carter said, "but I've been to the clinic this morning, and he's not going to die. Though I know people have been saying all over town that he is. Or that he already has, for God's sake."

"Well, why can't you just release my husband? Where is the judge?" It seemed to me that my mother's wish for Father's release, should it be granted, would help all this mess to blow over. Or at least help get it off the gossip mill.

Chief Carter assured my mother that holding her husband was more a formality than anything else. "The judge sent word, ma'am, that bond would be set as soon as the charges against the captain are known." My mother turned her head away.

"There were too many witnesses, Mrs. MacNee," Chief Carter said. "The captain agrees it'll play out better in the end if we're patient. Sentiment's building against the German. You mark my words, some people with the wrong-sounding last names, folks with a German accent, they're going to have a sorry row to hoe before this mess in Europe is over. That's their bad luck, and beyond my reach to fix. But, if we do this right, your husband will walk away from this no matter what."

"Can we just go back and see him now?" My mother stood, signaling an impatience I did not understand. "Let's go, Rove." It was almost as if she did not want my father turned loose. I could not have been more lost.

"Best thing for Captain MacNee when he does get out," Chief Carter said, nodding his head vigorously, "is for him to go straight to that boat of his and stay gone for about two weeks. Well, door's open, ma'am," Chief Carter said, hooking his thumb toward the gray metal door set in the opposite wall from his desk. "Captain'll like the home cooking you brought."

I guessed there was less than a feast in the basket: maybe two cold biscuits with sliced salt pork. Probably a wedge of pie left over from Granny Wooten's wake.

I opened the door for my mother and entered a few steps behind her. There were two cells facing the doorway through which we'd come, and one was vacant. In the other, in a high-backed, upholstered chair that was more appropriately a piece of furnishing from a tasteful den sat Dominus MacNee. The door to the cell was wide open.

His reading glasses were perched on his nose, his legs crossed, and a book open on his knee. He looked more like the professor than the sea captain. My mother and I stood in silence, as students or sailors might stand at the lectern or the helm, waiting. My father kept his eyes down, his finger on one of the book's pages, for time enough to finish the page he'd been reading when we came into his quarters.

And as my father read, the mental filter through which I viewed him softened and I saw a man who had once read to me from fat books off the shelves over his shoulder, strange and wondrous passages in a melodious voice as I sat cross-legged on the cushioned red carpet. I could have squinched my eyes and there would have appeared before me, that day in the cell, the man in whose arms I had awakened cradled and carried down the hall to my bed. I would close my eyes again and hold my head closer to my father's breast, to the strength that I knew would save me from every hurtful thing in the wide world.

I could feel my mother's eyes on me, and when I could not stop the tears from coming, I turned and walked out of the jail. I walked out past the chief, and walked out to the car, but not past what was hurting me. There didn't seem to be a road long enough down which I could walk, that would take me that far.

M*y mother made me* drive her straight from the jail to talk to the family's lawyer, Franklin J. Hollon. He had told her yesterday, she'd said, that his advice and counsel hinged on the outcome of the injuries Josef Unruh suffered. She did not tell me, as we made the short drive across town from the city jail to the lawyer's office, what else she wished to discuss with him.

And neither did I know then what Mr. Hollon might have said to Mother, but she walked slowly from his office and she frowned over something, some uncertainty perhaps. She even stopped once, and turned as if to go back inside. But then she had changed her mind again and whipped around, her dress flaring. She adjusted the pad at her shoulder, seeming uncomfortable in the fashion that gave her the squared-off shoulders of a woman dressed for church. The lawyer, years later, and drunk at an Elks Lodge picnic, told me she'd asked him that day about getting a divorce from my father, that she believed Dominus MacNee's mind was "alcohol poisoned."

Then, on the drive back home, my mother had fidgeted and looked mostly out the window. Then she reached over and tapped the steering wheel and told me to turn around and go back to the clinic at the other end of town. She might have told me that she wanted to dig up Granny Wooten and I would not have been more shocked when she said, "I want to ask after Mr. Unruh. I'll just be a minute," she said. "You can wait in the car."

"Mother, I don't want to go to see about him. I'm not going! I don't think it's right for you to go there, either."

"Rove MacNee! How dare you?"

I had never challenged my mother directly until that moment. "I dare, Mother, because you dare. Father is in jail for trying to kill a man," I said, my voice shaken by what would surely come when Dominus MacNee learned of this trip to the clinic. "And you want to go see how that man is doing?"

"You will not speak to me like that, young man." Mother had turned on the seat to face me. "Either drive the automobile as I wish, or get out and I'll drive myself." She switched her position and looked out the window for the rest of the ride to Anderson's Clinic. For my part, I don't know what I might have seen out the windshield of the Buick. I was completely removed from behind the wheel of the car and could not have told you if there'd been a caravan of circus elephants marching through Fair-hope. Instead of the street laid out in front of me, there was in front of my eyes the growing conviction that my mother had more than a passing interest in Josef Unruh. Though I was too naïve to produce more than mental sketches, the initial pictures were profound.

I tried, as I maneuvered the automobile, to drag my thoughts to a different place, but they were unyielding. I felt suddenly my stomach knotting in anger and confusion. I turned the big steering wheel and navigated the Buick into Dr. Anderson's bleached oyster shell parking lot. I stopped the car in the shade of a twisted old juniper and got out and went around and opened Mother's door. When I closed the door after her, she was already three steps toward the clinic.

"I'll let you drive home, Mother," I said, my voice firm. "I'm going to walk to the schoolhouse." I slammed the car door and walked across the parking lot without looking back in her direction.

It was lunchtime, and I thought I might find Anna Pearl outside on the campus lawn. I checked in at the Bell Building and told the secretary why I was late. I closed her office door and walked over to the big window by the potbelly stove. Someone had left it raised, and I thought to lower it since the black stove was fired up and working hard against the draft. I put my hand on the sill. The smell of winter caught up in the wind felt good bathing my face.

Then I saw Anna Pearl. She was sitting with two other girls on the back steps coming into the Bell Building. But what arrested me as completely as a fired-up, cloud-swirled sunset was that I could see past her knees underneath her dress. The light spring fabric, maybe white cotton, maybe a floral print, let the warm sunshine erase all the shadows between her knees, only just parted.

I was spiritually wounded as deeply in that moment as by some mythic gash administered by the fabled Fisher King himself. And, as the very breath was slipping in that moment from my body, I was in danger of falling onto my head, leaned, as my body was, out the window. Had I fallen, I'd have recovered well from my bruises. But from this other fall, I'm sure I still suffer some.

I raised my eyes by some inflowing of super strength to see Anna Pearl looking at me. And she did not press her knees together, and I could not look away. She smiled and got up and stepped away from her friends and waited for me. When I stood in front of her, she nodded toward a bench underneath a twisted old juniper beside the Bell Building.

"Let's sit down," she said.

I had not spoken to her since I stormed away from her at the funeral, and I couldn't get started with something to say. Anna Pearl cut her eyes away, a flush coming to her cheeks. I completely sidestepped the crazy brew of thoughts she'd inspired, just pushed it all aside and said, "I've been thinking about sailing away on the *Sea Bird*, and I was wondering if you thought your mother would approve me to graduate at the end of this year." Anna Pearl's face was round with surprise.

"What?" she asked, and after a pause, "What?"

As I let go a rush of words, trying to explain something that must have sounded preposterous, she at first seemed disbelieving, saying not a word. But soon enough, true to her ebullient nature, her eyes began to register a look of criminal conspiracy. I told her that I might not come back to school next year.

The ensuing conversation began with a flock of questions that flew from Anna Pearl:

"Where would you sail to? Can you captain a boat straight to the Straits of Gibraltar? Is there room for a sailor girl?"

On the last question, Anna Pearl lifted her eyebrows, formed a kiss on her lips, and gave her head a shake that sent her hair tumbling about her shoulders. I cut my eyes away, felt my face flush warm.

"Well, I—" I wasn't sure what to say. I looked at some of the other students passing nearby, who seemed to pay the two of us no mind. This girl could quicken my pulse with the least of her antics and attention.

"Why, Rove MacNee! All those foolish boys on their Sunday sloops just beg me to sit beside them on the windward side. But I believe I do detect some hesitation." She feigned a pouty face. "Oh, well, will you let me help you batten down the hatches, or whatever it is you sailors have to do before disappearing over the horizon?"

She seemed serious in her offer, so I told Anna Pearl that I could perhaps use her help, and that I would be grateful for the chance to get the work done on the boat faster.

"Plus, I would enjoy your company," I said, stealing a look her way, and, growing bolder, said, "I'll even take you sailing if you work hard."

"Aye, aye, sir," said Anna Pearl, who gave an open-fingered salute, and, dropping her hand back to her side, it seemed to me, as quick as that, she assumed a different demeanor entirely, and with a straight expression asked me if I really thought it would be okay to just leave school.

"Suppose you can't get the diploma at this point, Rove, will you still leave?"

"I don't know. But I think so," I said, becoming somber. "You saw what went on at my house Saturday."

"I could say to you that such things pass, but I couldn't mean it," she said. Her green eyes locked on mine, and I could see flecks of gold in the green. "Dominus MacNee means to kill that fellow, I do believe."

"And Josef Unruh means to defend himself. It's all so crazy to me."

I looked at a red-haired boy who had stopped near us and was staring in our direction. "Kid probably heard I'm the son of the knife-toting Blackbeard," I said. "And soon the marauder will be loose on the streets to strike terror in his little heart."

Anna Pearl paid no mind to what I'd said and went on following her thoughts.

"It's up to you, Rove," she said. "But, for my part, I think you should sail away. But won't you take this mess with you in your head?"

"Of course. But I think I can manage it from the Straits of Gibraltar better than I can from Magnolia Bayhouse."

"Well, I agree you've had enough schooling," Anna Pearl said. "Why, you might even know everything I know—well, *almost* everything I know. Anyway, Miss Anderson can approve your early graduation. Plus," she said, with a wink and a smile, "I could put in a word for you with her. On some days she's a good friend of my mine."

Her mother, headmistress at Organic School, had the authority to let me go with a diploma in hand. At Organic, students were not assigned to grades as such, but into four broad general groups called First Life, Second Life, Third Life, and Fourth Life. Students could also, by the book, advance to the next Life station when they were ready, with a teacher's approval and the agreement of the headmistress. Organic was altogether different from the public school. Educators from all over the world had come to see what Marietta Johnson had dreamed up and established in 1907 here in Fairhope. Some of the kids at the public school laughed at us for studying things like basket-weaving, but I loved the class and the way old Mrs. Harrison taught it. I used to think the public school should teach it, too, hire a Jicarilla Apache woman for the teacher with a chisel-faced warrior at her side to club down the snickers.

At Organic, we had no homework, there were no tests, and the teachers got students to learn by helping to stir up curiosity and desire. We even got a glimpse of the different world of work and on Wednesdays prepared and served lunches for the townspeople in the school cafeteria, and put on skits and other performances during the meal.

Anna Pearl's friend, white-haired and long-whiskered old Henry Stuart, who teaches us rug-weaving on an H-loom on Tuesdays, always came to the Wednesday lunches, never missed, no matter the weather. He walked to town, always barefoot, from his hideaway round concrete hut that looked something like an igloo, hidden on ten acres the old man calls Tolstoy Park—a few miles north of town. At least once a school year for the last four, we'd taken class field trips to see Mr. Stuart.

When he came to Organic for the lunches, Mr. Stuart took his plate and sat alone, unless Anna Pearl sat with him. He'd pat his bare feet to the folk music rhythms we students raised from homemade instruments.

Anna Pearl told me she'd like for me to get to know him better, and when I declined, saying there were enough people in my head at the moment, she got angry.

"That is just such a strange thing to say, Rove," she'd said. "People don't live in your head. What makes you think anyone would allow you to claim them like that? It's silly, if not arrogant."

Then she'd added with a bit of a huff, "The best part of school just might be the people we meet, the friends we make, the scrapes we get into and out of with real people, Rove. We don't come to this place every day to just bury our heads in books, or fumble to make a basket, for heaven's sake."

I said nothing, didn't argue that people take over rooms and corners in my own mind. The more I love them, the louder, the more notorious their presence becomes. And when they leave, like Grandpa Otis and Granny Wooten, the silence in their wake is deafening.

In those days, my father was such a dissonant thrum in

my head, with such growing volume and intensity, that I had no room left to know another soul.

For me, it is the soul of a man that confronts me in the deeper bonds of friendship. Soul, with enough substance to cast a shadow, to greater or lesser degrees. And though I could not understand clearly the workings of Captain Dominus MacNee, in this man I had drawn for a father I felt the chill of the shadow behind his soul, and felt it more acutely as days passed, and in the shadow was something as cold and as deep as Emily Dickinson's zero at the bone.

"If the war continues," I said to Anna Pearl, "maybe I'd even join the navy. It would be an expense-paid ticket out of town."

"Doesn't shooting at people and people shooting back at you give you some pause?" Anna Pearl asked with her eyebrows up high.

I did not think of myself as a warrior, nor even as particularly patriotic, when compared with the zeal of my father. But news and rumors from Europe about Nazi deeds were chilling and evocative of scary sermons about endtimes.

"If I think about it, yes," I allowed. "But an army working for a man like Hitler has to be met and stopped."

It seemed certain in my mind that Germany was going to keep up its provocations until the United States declared war on the Nazis. Talk at the barbershop deemed it a certainty. Some kids at school parroted the panic issuing from their parlors and supper tables at home.

"I know," Anna Pearl said. "It was spooky to me when President Roosevelt last summer ordered all the German consulates closed. Did you read that piece about Mobile's German vice-consul, Walter Zingelmann? He left town ahead of the official expulsion, you know. The story in the newspaper said his letter canceling his subscription was signed 'Heil Hitler.' "

"One thing's for sure," I added. "My father would drape my shoulders with the Stars and Stripes as he escorted me to the bus station."

"And what if you're completely wrong about that, Rove? What about your mother? Don't you think she'd have something to say about you going off to war?"

"Well, she might." I paused and looked at my knees. "I guess she would. But come next October I'll be seventeen, and I can volunteer to serve aboard a U.S. ship without anybody's consent. Including the school's. Swabbing decks and loading big guns doesn't take a high school diploma."

Next morning I decided to cut class and go instead down to the *Sea Bird*. I almost never skipped school, and the Organic teachers wouldn't complain under the circumstances. History lessons would just now be commencing. Besides rug-weaving with Mr. Stuart, it was the only class I shared with Anna Pearl. She'd wonder where I was, I guessed, and might even think to look for me at the boat after school. I could only hope.

I hadn't made up my mind to go to the creek until I found myself almost at school, walking through Fairhope. A friend of my father raised his hand to me from the porch of McKean's Hardware as I passed. Behind him, standing between two other men, was Jimmy Davis in his army uniform. He'd been called Smokey in school because he was so willing to get into a fight. *Where there's smoke, there's fire,* someone was likely to say when Jimmy tore into an adversary after school. Smokey had joined the army last year when he graduated, after a summer of fishing and sailing and chasing the girls, and had gone to boot camp in August sometime. I guessed he must have been on the short leave soldiers get between completing basic training and getting their permanent duty assignment.

"Hey, MacNee!" Smokey said, stepping through the circle of men. "You going to be laying out of school, you oughta cinch up your girlie drawers and go join the army. They'll make a man out of you, if you don't get your pecker shot off."

Smokey forced a raspy laugh and looked left and right at the men who grinned and clapped him on the shoulder. The man who knew my father, whose name I did not know, laid the back of his hand on the shoulder of Jimmy Davis and pushed him aside with little effort. Smokey frowned at the man, who returned the look with an open, flat face that telegraphed authority, and then nodded to me.

I nodded, said nothing, and turned north on Section Street, keeping to that street all the way out of town, with my eyes down and my hands in my pockets as I went. My father was at home. Chief Carter had let him go yesterday, and he'd walked in the door at Magnolia Bayhouse just at suppertime. With Granny Wooten's death at Thanksgiving, and my father's jail release three weeks before Christmas, 'twas not quite the season to be jolly. Father and Mother had avoided each other like some quarantine had been established for them by the doctor. When I left for school this morning, he had been packing his grip to set sail on the *Mary Foster*.

"This will be a quick run," he'd told my mother, breaking the evening's truce of silence. He cut his eyes at me. "Just something to keep me below the horizon until Lady Justice puts aside her spyglass."

I stopped still for a moment and stared at the bundle of clothes in his hands.

"Oh, would that Justice were truly blind," he said, feigning something of a histrionic voice. "I'd get my business done without skulking about."

Then the captain announced to us, but more to the room than to either Mother or me specifically, that he'd sent word to his men two days ago from the jail to make the *Mary Foster* ready. "We'll be filling our hold with fresh fish in Bayou La Batre. Two days to New Orleans, a day in port, and two days back."

The captain told me to mind things about Magnolia Bayhouse for Mother. "You keep an eye out for the German. He's on his feet again and he might try to pull something while I'm gone. Be wary. Don't be a soldier caught sleeping."

And then, before either Mother or I had made good sense of the captain's flurry of words and actions about the house, he was gone. And I had walked to school in something of a daze, and found I had no mind for studies.

This campaign of Dominus MacNee against Josef Unruh had actually taken hold in the community. I knew it was a consequence of the mood of rising anger over Hitler's defiance, the spittle-spraying rage of a dictator who meant to seat himself above human decency, above any regard for innocence, above any voice contrary to his purposes. To the good people of Fairhope and America, Hitler seemed a stand-up version of the evil that preachers warned of in their Sunday sermons.

But Josef Unruh was not Adolf Hitler. He was a man, not a country. He was innocent, until proven guilty. I knew the very law of the nation hung on the premise of such basic personal liberty.

I could only hope the nervous vigilantes would not direct their queries about the German in their midst to me, assuming I was something on the order of second-in-command by virtue of blood inheritance of the captain's rage. There was simply no way that I was going to go through a school day of quizzing and stares, and found I was calmed by the prospects of having the creek and my boat to myself.

An easy rain began to fall. I walked Section Street, meeting no cars or other walkers. The street ran straight as a bowstring over low hills short and long from a few miles south of the town limits to a couple miles north of where it crossed Fairhope Avenue at the center of town. I made my way past shops and stores and houses. At the north end of town, still walking along Section Street, the rain had stopped falling. When I cut into the woods, I pushed the water out of my hair with both hands and stopped to listen. There's a softness in the air that follows a rain, like the respectful silence that follows when the priest dips his chin in prayer, and the slope down to the creek brought no sound back up to me. I was careful, too, that my footfalls were quiet as I stepped through the copse of camphor and sweet bay and juniper that stood wet and gray and silent on the hillside. My breathing ballooned little fog clouds into the chilly morning and the quiet in the woods.

I soon came into view of the *Sea Bird* where she was moored broadside to the bank, bobbing in the gentle current with her heavy docklines sagging lazily between twin sycamores and the sloop's Sampson post and her stern cleats. I stopped several steps short of the water's edge to admire my boat. She was a beauty, her classic sheer and wineglass-shaped transom a delight to the eye. Her sharply raked mast and five-foot bowsprit suggested speed and grace. *Sea Bird* had come to my mind for a name without any fishing about or waffling on the choice. And, since Mr. Unruh had not ever named his boat—the only boat I'd ever known without a name—I didn't have to risk the sailor's superstition about changing a boat's name. I painted the name on the transom myself within a month of the gift of her to me. Black letters, with only a little flourish at the serifs, with gold leaf shading.

The cabin roof was low for seaworthiness and better handling in a squall, while the sloop's four-foot draft and eight-foot beam permitted a comfortable main salon with full standing headroom belowdecks and a spacious forepeak berth. The soft smell of the seasoned wood in the cozy cabin, with hints of seawater from the bilge, and the faint aroma of lamp oil all blended together to float through the space like incense at the mass I sometimes visited. I wondered what the priest would say about my moving out of Magnolia Bayhouse, thought he'd probably advise against it, but perhaps halfheartedly and with a twinkle of envy in his lively brown eyes.

What had it been now? Almost two years? The first weeks of owning the *Sea Bird* had flown past for me. Almost every afternoon after school I'd come down to work on her and spruce her up, often with Josef Unruh's help. I was surprised some afternoons to find the German already at the boat. I was glad for his company as well as his expert advice. But he was not a garrulous man and, in fact, I remember whole afternoons of work with half a dozen sentences spoken. Sometimes Father Brown would show up and pitch in for an hour or so, and those were the most talkative times.

I had acquired skill working with wood and tools in my father's shop, but what I knew did not translate directly to boat carpentry. The curves and compound curves of the boat's ribs were extremely difficult for me to pattern and cut. The three cracked ribs I'd found I'd repaired with "sisters," new wood on either side of the damaged ribs that had taken me two months of brief spans of hours and a couple of half-days to screw into place.

Josef Unruh had come to Fly Creek with his heavy, hinged toolbox, its top tray filled with an assortment of knives and saws and bits, little jars with screws and nails, a small mallet, and a big brass hammer, and when we worked together, he had pushed me to find solutions to problems.

"Vat is ze value of so much telling zees and zat. You

tell me: How vill you fix ze cracked rib? Zat is learning, ja." He spoke sternly, and my jaw was tightening in response, but then he winked.

I found myself liking Mr. Unruh, looking forward to the times when he showed up to help. I was not unmindful of the transference at play, how the power of the emotions were lifted straight from my feelings for my father. The day Mr. Unruh showed me how to scribe a curve onto a paper pattern using a spacer block and a fat pencil was so very much like working with my father in his woodshop, for my father, too, loved to show me woodworking techniques. He treated them like old family secrets, and when I "got it" he nodded in a way that signaled a kind of complicity. The nod, I think, was my father's version of Mr. Unruh's wink.

Days would pass, too, when I worked alone, and it was satisfying to be on the creek with no one else around.

Mr. Unruh's westernmost property line fronted about three hundred feet of this remote stretch of Fly Creek, with thirty acres rising behind the creek, up and over several hills, running east across Section Street. In the middle of his land was a high piney ridge, and there was his stucco cottage and a windmill, up the hill to the right side of Section Street just where I had turned left. Mr. Unruh's front door was maybe a half mile off the bay.

I rarely saw another person on the creek near my moorage, had seen only two skiffs come around the bend, blue exhaust drifting up from their outboards into the pines and magnolias and cypresses. One of the fishermen had raised his hand in greeting as I passed in the *Sea Bird,* though no one from either of the skiffs had spoken to me. I didn't mind the solitude of the creek. Only sometimes I wished for another pair of hands for this or that task, but managed one way or the other by myself.

Heeling the boat at low tide to expose hull seams for caulking, however, was a task that required Mr. Unruh's help, which he offered easily. We had strung the main halyard from the mast to a tall, silver-barked poplar and hauled the sloop over on its side, its keel stuck in the sand and mud of a high spot in the creek near the bank.

"I believe ve will find solid planking below ze waterline," Mr. Unruh said. "Your inspection in ze bilges was good, ja?" I said that I'd found no soft wood while poking around with his awl.

"Still, it is necessary to recaulk every ten years or so. Ze oakum caulking, if ve find it is still good, can be tapped deeper into ze seam," Mr. Unruh said, "and ve vill add more strands on top, then swipe on new bottom paint. If ze oakum is rotten, ve have to dig it out and redo ze seam." I was lucky. The caulking was good, and we did not have to do the more extensive bottom work.

On another day we turned the boat around and did the other side. Josef Unruh would rather work in silence, but when we would take a break, he talked freely to me about his hours spent under sail aboard the boat, about how much he preferred her sloop rig to a yawl or schooner.

We had already gone back to work one day when I asked, "Why did you quit sailing her?"

Mr. Unruh said nothing and tapped more strands of oakum into the exposed seams. When there came no quick reply, I looked up from my mallet and chisel work and was interested to see Mr. Unruh momentarily still and looking intently at the piece of oakum he was working. His boots sucked in the mud as he shifted his feet. If he had been a schoolmate, I'd say the teacher had caught him out on something and he was sanguinely framing a good reply.

"I became too busy, I suppose," he finally said, and then changed the subject with a smile. And put the entire matter to rest with: "I hope ve have enough bottom paint to give two coats to our good work."

We soon finished and painted on a first coat. I came the next day at low tide and put on a heavy second coat. Josef Unruh had not been home when I'd come to the creek. Nor was he home the next two days, but before the week was out, I managed at high tide to kedge and winch my boat back into the creek's deep water and retie her mooring lines.

We worked together only one other time after the caulking. Maybe three months ago, just at the end of summer. I was surprised that dog-day morning when he began speaking of the "terror and tragedy being wrought by zis maniac." I had learned not to expect Joseph Unruh to talk and his comments were unsolicited. "All uff ze Germans vill be marked with Hitler's infamy." I had not responded, had caught his inference that he would be among the Germans "marked," and he looked at me and said only, "The shame vill be exceeded only by pain."

Then Mr. Unruh had crawled into the forepeak to inspect the stem and had come out saying only that it was in good shape. He said the work on the boat was almost finished, that it was well done. "You vill luff to sail her," he said, and left the creek. His limp seemed more pronounced that day walking up the short hill through the woods toward Section Street. Or perhaps I was only looking with more focus and purpose.

The captain did not like the gift of the boat to me, made no bones about it. But he would not forbid me to work on it, said nothing a man did on a boat could be wrong, and now and again he had actually asked me how the work was going.

Once, when I was nine, I had asked my father when he might get a sailboat "for playing," adding that the *Mary Foster* was too big. The captain's answer had come without hesitation, and around a big laugh: "When you can acquire one for yourself, by any means short of stealing it, you may have a sailboat. Even if that is this afternoon."

And with the *Sea Bird*, I had done that. And the captain, whatever else he was, was a man of his word to his son. If the captain said the two of us would go fishing on Saturday, even if a driving rain decided, too, upon that day for its business, we would go fishing.

"Dominus, what is the point of going out into this?" my mother had once complained. "You will not catch a fish and you know it."

"And my son will learn when the fish bite, and when

the fish do not bite." Then he'd crossed his arms and looked at me, adding, "And we will perhaps learn that fish do what fish wish to do without regard for our expectations." And with a smile for his wife, turning to her and pointing at her with his pipe, said, "So keep your spices at the ready, woman!"

We had not caught a fish on that outing, but I could not remember a fishing trip with my father that filled me with greater hope of bringing home the big one. Nor could I remember a wetter one. Clear memories of circumstances like the weather marked my cravings for company with the captain, for the captain to be my father and not the captain.

Like the nip in the wind from the season's first northerly when I told my father that I was almost ready to shake down the *Sea Bird.* It was the first week of October and Granny Wooten was still getting about, though slowly. She'd even puttered around in the kitchen that morning, feebly trying to help Mother with breakfast. Over my father's third cup of coffee, just the two of us out on the gallery, I'd told him I was ready to take the *Sea Bird* out into the bay for my first sail aboard her. The captain, clear-eyed and relaxed, had clapped me on the back and walked out onto the pier in front of Magnolia Bayhouse. He talked to me about the sail-handling I had learned aboard the *Mary Foster.* He complimented my confidence and speed with the halyards and sheets, my agility in moving about on a wave-tossed and rolling deck. He spoke proudly of how once I had foreseen and prevented an accidental jibe of the mainsail that could have ripped the mast out of the deck, so hard was the wind blowing that day.

"That was quite a storm, son, but you were sailor enough to match it. I tell you, that day I did not see a boy playing about on the deck of my boat. I saw a man at work," the captain said.

I was drawn into the moment with my father and said that he should come along on the sloop's maiden voyage. The captain became silent for a full minute, looking at me, at the horizon almost wistfully, and back at me. A smile broke onto my face, so excited was I that my father might consent to sail with me on the *Sea Bird*.

"Mr. Unruh and I are going down to the creek on Saturday, and—" I was not even allowed to finish my sentence before my father said, "To hell with him!" and stomped off the dock without another word.

Though I had been thinking I would live on the boat until summer, when school let out, and then sail away, now I was considering setting out before my father came home. Soon after Mr. Unruh had given the boat to me, I had taken down from my father's bookshelves the volume by Joshua Slocum, *Sailing Alone Around the World*. I had read with intense interest the accounts of Captain Joshua's single-handed voyage around the world in a rebuilt derelict hundred-year-old oyster boat, a sloop given the name *Spray*.

I had taken note of the book in my father's library, but now that I owned my own sloop, I was keen to read about the voyage of the *Spray*. Working without power tools in 1892, the self-reliant Slocum had done all the repair and makeover work to his boat by himself. He was almost fifty when he set sail. Slocum spent three years and two months circumnavigating the world in his thirty-seven-foot boat.

I became aware that while standing back admiring the *Sea Bird*, I'd absentmindedly struck a pose, arms crossed and feet wide apart, like my father. I didn't feel like a high school student at all, and if the sun had broken through the clouds and flung down my shadow onto the leafy ground, it would have cut a figure easily distinguished as a sailorman, and a single sentence from Joshua Slocum now burned in my mind: "To young men contemplating a voyage I would say go."

Satisfied that my boat was almost, but not quite, ready and seaworthy for anything I had in mind, I stepped alongside her, careful to avoid the mud so I didn't track it onto the deck. I bent over and took hold of a dock line and hauled in on it so the *Sea Bird* nudged herself over to allow me aboard.

I loved the gentle dip of the deck when I stepped onto it and the soft lap of the water as it rippled out toward the middle of the creek from the curve of the sloop's hull at the waterline. As I moved about on deck, the *Sea Bird* rocked easily and the ripples in the creek rolled all the way to the other bank.

I would need now to lay onto the *Sea Bird* basic stores, to load down my little sloop with coffee and beans, and—what else? Certainly my mullet net. I would make a list. And I had ignored certain repairs and improvements to the standing and running rigging on the *Sea Bird,* her stays and halyards and sheets and sails. One winch was sticky. Both the mainsail and the jib needed some little restitching. I'd get busy and make the sloop completely ready, "shipshape and Bristol fashion" as Josef Unruh had recommended. I'd get *Sea Bird* ready to take out of Mobile Bay. Anna Pearl had insisted on helping me. So I would let her, and with the extra help I would be ready to go all the sooner.

Brushing puddled rainwater from the cockpit seat, I sat down at the tiller. I put my hand on the oaken lever that moved the big rudder hanging on the stern. I moved the tiller away from myself, felt the resistance of the water on the broad blade, pulled it back, and smiled at how easily that little fanning of the rudder, like a fish's tail, moved the sloop forward some few inches until she tightened up on her dock line.

I looked forward along the deck, following the curving gunwale with my eye, the gentle upsweep of the *Sea Bird*'s sheer. From where I sat, looking forward, it seemed to me that all the lines the naval architect had drawn for the design of this vessel swept sensually forward to the tip of the bowsprit. Her *finishing point.* And yet from there, the sabre tip of her being was thrust into the open sea.

Yes, I will go. My courage and confidence were growing.

In my mind's eye, I went up high. Up above the tree-tops, up to brush the clouds, and I saw as from the eye of an osprey this Fly Creek, a twisting, winding vein of freshwater that quietly emptied into Mobile Bay from her eastern shore in the town of Fairhope where I had been born.

And I saw below me the Eastern Shore, known by locals as the narrow crescent of Alabama land hugging Mobile Bay, from Spanish Fort sitting on a heavily wooded bluff to the north, and stretching south for about twenty miles to the turn-of-the-century bayfront mansions south of the Grand Hotel at Great Point Clear. And I saw from up there the bristle of private docks and finger piers all along the shore.

The seagulls and brown pelicans could look down on the boats in the harbors, might even hear the ruckus of schoolchildren in their play yards, merchants outside their stores, neighbors gossiping at fences.

Then I brought my reverie into a free fall, down and down, to the wavetops and my little sloop running ahead of a fresh northerly at a ten-degree angle of heel, the wind off my starboard quarter and a great *whoosh* in my ears and the whole scene of the town falling quickly from view behind the stern of the *Sea Bird*. Here in this idle fantasy, though I did not know it at the time, was the birth of a dream that would echo across countless nights.

I curled my fingers tight around the tiller. I sat up straight-backed and laughed aloud to the silent denizens thereabouts, "Yes, Granny Wooten, sometimes boys do find themselves following a bowsprit past the end of their noses."

I'd *stayed aboard* my sloop until nearly dark and was past supper getting home. Mother tried to get me to eat something and said she'd set a plate for me, but I declined and went to bed. Sleep did not come easily around my decision to start packing in the morning, but soon enough I was awakened by a call to breakfast. When I didn't soon show up in the kitchen, Mother came to my room, stopping abruptly at the door, still wiping her hands on her apron.

"Excuse me. What is this you're doing?"

I didn't answer. Instead I put a pair of boots into the bottom of the bag, my grip, the very same one of heavy cotton duck I'd packed so many times to sail out on the *Mary Foster* with my father. Then I told Mother I was going to stay on my boat.

"Rove, do you really believe your father is going to allow you to move out of this house?" Underclothes went next into the bag. I laid in three books: *The Adventures of Huckleberry Finn,*

Sailing Alone Around the World, and my logbook, with its holographic title *Voyage of the Sea Bird.*

My mother was now following behind me each step around my room, her fists on her hips, hovering near when I would stoop to pick up this or that item for stuffing into my canvas bag. "Rove, please talk to me," she said.

"Mother, I'm not looking for his permission to do this," I said, feigning intense concentration on what I would next toss into my grip. Actually, I was packing sloppily, I was so distracted with my mother's busy proximity.

Finally, I sat heavily on my well-made bed and plopped the bag onto the floor at my feet. "No, I don't expect Father will like this at all," I said. "Granny Wooten does not care a whit, though. Does she?" I gripped the bedclothes beside my thighs, and my knuckles whitened and tears came to my eyes, but I blinked them away and set my jaw.

My mother's face softened. She turned and drew the little Windsor chair over near the bed and sat down. She folded her hands in her lap.

"I know it has been hard on you, Rove, to lose your grandmother." She reached out and patted my knee. "It's not easy to bid final good-byes. She loved you so much, from the day you were born."

My mother looked away, out the window, and still without looking my way, her voice hardening, said, "It does not help the way your father has been drinking, and all these crazy outbursts." Then she looked at me, a frown pinching her face.

"Mother, it's not that this has been hard on me. I don't feel singled out here." I stared straight into her gray eyes. "What about Julian?" I let the question hang a long minute. "And what about you? She was your mother. We're all breathing the same family air here." My father's name popped up on the list, but I said nothing and stood up quickly and turned toward the window.

Outside a little morning's breeze had begun to play on the bay, just rippling the surface so that the dark water had the texture of Arabian sand dunes like those I saw in my geography text. Farther out and north toward Mobile, the wind pushed harder and agitated the water into a light chop that would soon spread to the water at the end of our dock. I have seen the waters of Mobile Bay change expression in a half hour, the former face unrecognizable to the latter. The same thing can happen to a man, or even a boy.

"And poor Mr. Unruh. He could have been killed."

I spun around. "I don't give a damn about Mr. Unruh. I can't believe you'd bring up his name."

"Rove MacNee!"

I went back and sat on my bed and bent forward, resting my forearms on my thighs, my face down. I stared at a knot on the pineboard floor between my shoes.

"You say Mr. Unruh could have been killed, but what about my father?" I sat up straight and looked at my mother. "What about him? What's happening to him?"

I got up again and walked past my mother, back over to

the tall window. I blew my breath on the wavy pane of glass at eye level, and on the frosted surface I drew quickly with my finger a profile of a pelican in flight, a doodle I loved to do. Just three lines, actually: one for the broad-breasted body and head with the prominent fishing beak, and one line for each wing, fanned at the tips like feathers. I wiped it all away with my sleeve and turned to face my mother.

"You keep saying, and I keep thinking, that it's the drinking. But, could there be something else going on? Is there a better explanation?"

My mother's eyes fluttered and her gaze danced rapidly away. She stood up and returned the chair to its place near the window, beside me. She put her hand on my shoulder, but withdrew it.

"What else would it be, Rove? Some men just fall into a bottle. It could have been predicted that your father would. Your paternal grandfather was a profaning sot."

I looked at her, projecting my disdain for the line she was taking. My hands at my sides reflexively curled into fists, but when my mother looked at me, I opened my palms and straightened my fingers. There is no way she could have known that what I heard sounded to my ears like a curse laid on my head, that I would someday fall prey to drink.

"If your father poured his whiskey down the drain, none of this would be happening. All of this foolish paranoia and these accusations and violent behavior would swirl away."

She walked to the door and took the doorknob in her hand and stopped and looked back at me. "Do you think your father can stop drinking, Rove? No. You know it's hopeless, and that's why you're leaving. But what am I to do?"

"I have no idea what's going to happen," I said. "I just know what I have to do."

"I don't blame you for moving out, Rove. If there were somewhere I could go—" I could tell from the defeat that echoed from her words that she believed her way out of Magnolia Bayhouse had been cut off, that she was inside and the doors were locked on the outside. There was nowhere sensible for her and Julian to go. I felt my mother's desperation and I wished I could do something. I hinted that maybe I'd come back home soon.

"Let's just call this a practice run, Mother." She looked at me. "Maybe I won't like camping on a small boat."

My mother looked upward and tapped her forehead as if studying something important. Her voice was bright. "I expect I would allow you to come home." She lifted her eyebrows in a hint of mischief. "If you slink in the door properly repentant for abandoning me here in this suffocating foolishness."

I smiled and my mother smiled back at me.

"So I'll go and try my hand at spending some nights on the boat in the creek. Let's just leave it at that for now. And when Father comes home," I lifted my hands and shrugged, "well—I'll adjust my plans as I need to. If you need me, I'll be here. Is that okay, Mother?"

"No." Mother shook her head, serious. "If I were you, literally, if it was me who had a boat ready to sail, I would load all I could right now into the trunk of the car, and I would take myself and my things to that pretty boat, and I would untie the lines and stand on the deck and wave to Mother and little brother."

She stood by the window at my shoulder. "Just look at the way the wind plays on the bay and the sun shines on this beautiful Friday morning." She tapped the glass in front of me. "I haven't seen a lovelier day in weeks, and I cannot imagine a better time for Rove MacNee to take over the helm of his own fate." She nodded playfully. "Do you like that seafaring metaphor?"

"I do, Mother. And, actually, there's a poem with a line very close to that. It goes, 'I am the master of my fate: I am the captain of my soul.' "

"So see how close to the muse is your dear mother."

I did not tell her that the rest of William E. Henley's poem describes an awful world black as a pit, a place of wrath and tears that subjects unwitting souls to the bludgeonings of chance, and whose only hope resides in taking full and complete responsibility for the life-course we sail.

My mother strode purposefully out of the room and down the hall, humming a Harry James melody, maybe a Frank Sinatra number. She stopped and came back to my door to say she would pack some food for me. In her voice I heard something of the excitement that was building in my own chest, now that the difficult cat of my leaving had been let out of the bag in my mother's house.

I turned to the window, framing so that selfsame world where I had walked within the past hour, unmindful then of the way the sunlight reflected off the trees' silvery parchment of rough winter bark.

Here on the coast, some insistent waxen green always flagged the leaves with a counterpoint promise of spring. The wind blew steadily now, and the bay was a white-fractured blue reflection of the cloudless sky. A mullet flew from the water twenty yards out past the end of the pier, trailing watery beads in its arc. Then another jump, and another. I had time. It would be good to pitch my net before going to the creek.

I called out to my mother that I was headed for the pier, and I went out the front door, across the gallery at a quick pace, and to the bottom of the steps, where I flipped away the cypress board covering my mullet net in the galvanized bucket. I grabbed up the bucket by its bail and made for the dock. I'd sure take my net and bucket with me aboard the *Sea Bird* after this brief fishing. Julian had been playing with Elberta at the corner of the house. The little dog loved to chase sticks for Julian, though she was reluctant to relinquish her prize to him and she growled while they did their tug-of-war. Julian turned loose his end of the stick and trotted after me.

"You see something, Rove?"

"Supper. Maybe."

"Can I come with you?"

"Looks like you mean to do that. Sure. Just don't walk down the dock like an elephant." I looked back at Elberta, prancing onto the boards with the stick still in her mouth, intent, perhaps, on getting her game started up again. "And try to keep Elberta quiet. Every fish from here to Mobile will head for deeper water if she starts a fuss."

"She won't cut up unless I grab hold of her stick, and I won't do that. So can I throw the net?"

I turned and looked back at my brother. "Didn't Father Brown give you a net, Julian?"

"He said he had a bait net I could start with, but he didn't bring it to me yet."

"Okay, okay. Let me fill up my bucket, and I'll give you a turn with the net." I kept looking back over my shoulder at the big grin spread across my brother's face, at how Julian also never combed his hair, and how I saw the same few freckles across my brother's nose that I looked at each morning in the shaving mirror. "Hey, Julian. I'm going to be taking some stuff down to the sailboat in a while. Maybe you'd like to ride down there with me."

If it was possible, my brother's face lit up even more. He bent over and patted Elberta on the head, as if to share his good luck with her. The dog lay on her belly, chewing her stick, ignoring us both. Julian stood up. "I'd like to do that. Sure. You want to take our bicycles down to the creek?"

"No, we'll just take the Buick. Mother said I could use it."

I turned my attention back toward the end of the pier, didn't need to watch Julian's face to read the pleasure registered there. I didn't have to say anything more to my little brother. I knew that in all likelihood not much else would be said between us for the balance of the afternoon, as the two of us made our rounds doing what brothers do when they are just knocking around together.

Late in the afternoon Julian and I took the Buick and some things I'd packed into two small canvas bags—kerosene for my hanging lamp in the main salon, a short list of hardware items like matches and a glass jar of bronze boat nails, and two wool blankets—and stowed them aboard the *Sea Bird*.

We drove home with Julian chattering like a squirrel the whole way about all manner of things. Except the bombing at Pearl Harbor yesterday. Julian was blissfully ignorant of its catastrophic implications for our country and all the lives in it, including his. He asked me if I thought Father might get a dog for him, "one bigger than Elberta," and I told him he should probably wait until his birthday to ask for a dog. That would be in the summer, and things should be cooler by then.

But I didn't say that to Julian. There would have been something about summer being hot, not cool, and there would be the moment when I'd say it was a figure of speech, and he would ask what's a figure of speech and I'd let the whole thing drop by changing the subject. And then I'd spend some more time thinking that Julian maybe deserved to be closer inside the family dynamic, not left on the periphery of the truth about war. Easier just to put it off. Maybe I'd be gone by his birthday. And such was as good as Julian got from the captain and his mother and me back then.

When he and I had walked into the parlor after coming home from church yesterday, Mother was sitting in her sewing chair dragged up in front of the big radio, her face in her hands, crying. The forward curl of her body looked almost fetal and she rocked slightly back and forth. The announcer's voice was so frantic and forlorn he could have been a radio play actor, and I made no sense of his report. Something about the unbelief and horror. But as I listened and my mind wobbled into sync with the announcer's voice, I heard him say the bomb that hit the USS *Arizona* had penetrated the hull and caused massive explosions. So enormous and devastating was the damage, the radio report said, that the ship and its crew immediately sank to the bottom of the harbor.

"A grave has been made of an entire ship," the announcer said.

Mother looked up, her eyes red and her face a mess, and said, "Take your brother outside." I did not, only told him to go find Elberta, and did not leave the room. I had to scold Julian to get him moving, and he stomped out and slammed the door in his wake.

Twenty minutes later I went outside and told him, in

a voice a mile away from me, that America had been bombed by the Japanese. He squatted and scratched Elberta between her ears and asked if we would bomb them back and I said that we would and he had said, "It's okay then."

As I slowed the Buick to turn into our drive, I looked over at Julian, who carefully watched the world rolling past his car window, satisfied that it was okay, then. It was true, after all, what I'd told him about bombing them back. The Congress had made my prophecy official when they declared war, first on the Imperial government of Japan, and three days later on Germany and Italy. President Roosevelt had addressed them, and us, saying that the day our country was suddenly and deliberately attacked would live in infamy. They had bombed us and we were going to bomb them back.

I put my arm out the window to signal my left turn and saw in the mirror Chief Carter close behind me in his police car. He flashed his headlights. I made my turn onto our shell driveway and stopped the car. He pulled in behind me and parked and got out. As he walked toward us, Julian was up on his knees looking backward and said, "God, Rove. What did you do?"

My voice was unsteady when I said I had done nothing, running a list in my head: speeding, no brake lights, something about Father.

"Good day, boys." Chief Carter bent at the waist and looked into the car, first at me, then at Julian. "Rove, could you step back to my car for a minute?"

Julian, for once, had nothing to say, and I couldn't have said anything if I'd wanted to as I followed Chief Carter to his patrol car. He opened the door and took an envelope off the dashboard.

"I went to Josef Unruh's place, kind of a follow-up, you know, and he gave me this. Asked me to give it to you." I took the envelope and thanked Chief Carter. I could tell that he wanted me to open it so he could know what was inside, but I folded the envelope in half and put it into my back pocket, looking to see if Julian was watching through the back window of the car. He was. I said good-bye to the police chief and thanked him again.

When I got in the car, Julian asked, "What did he give you?"

"A note from the school." And he was completely satisfied with the lie.

I parked the car and we went inside. I told Mother that I would go back to the boat while there was still plenty of daylight so I could get things put in order there. I stood on the porch and said good-bye to my mother and brother. The envelope in my back pocket was like a living thing and I could feel it breathing and its heart beating. It looked as though Mother might start to cry. "I'm only going a few miles across town," I said. "Please, don't worry."

And that made her tears turn loose. My brother said, "You don't have to cry, Mother." Julian turned to look at me. "If he needs us, he'll come straight home. Right, Rove?"

"Yes, Julian," I said, hugging him as I said to my mother, "It's all right, Mother. Really."

"Of course it is, Son. I'm just—well, all the news coming in on the radio and—" She looked at Julian, and then in a stronger voice said to me, "Just never mind all that. You get on back to your boat, and Julian and I will come and see you tomorrow." She cocked her head and raised her eyebrows. "I assume we may visit?" she said, making a question of it, putting on a smile.

"Of course." And with that, and brief hugs for both my mother and brother, I mounted my bicycle and set off for Fly Creek, my thoughts spinning faster than the spoked wheels beneath me. And spinning faster than all the others: my own dismay that when my mother said "we," I saw not her and Julian, but Lillian MacNee and Josef Unruh walking down the slope toward *Sea Bird*. I pumped the bicycle pedals hard, and harder, until the sweat on my neck and back helped salve the knocking behind my eyes and the catch in my throat. The envelope tingled so in my back pocket that I stopped and put down the kickstand, and slipped the bent and creased white envelope out and took a breath while staring at it, then opened it.

Inside was a photograph with scalloped edges, just smaller than a playing card. The picture was sharp, the image clear and focused: Josef Unruh sailing on an easy reach in the sloop I'd named the *Sea Bird*. The photographer must have been on a nearby boat. The man at the tiller was smiling and waving for the camera, as all good photo subjects should. I refused to study the picture, thinking it might, like the white man's camera, capture something of my soul. I put it back into the envelope and into my shirt pocket. I had no idea what I'd do with it.

In Fairhope, passing the drugstore at the corner of Section Street and Fairhope Avenue, I saw Father Brown and invited him to come down for a visit aboard the *Sea Bird*. I might ask for his shoulder. Not to cry on, but for a place to rest, and I hoped he might say things that would raise my spirits. Is that not what he suited up for every morning? The priest said he'd be there in an hour and, in fact, showed up not ten minutes after I got aboard.

My respect for Father Brown grew out of a regard for him that I felt strongly at our first meeting. Something about him put me at ease; something about him invited me to trust him; something about him encouraged me to believe that he knew what he was talking about, maybe even spoke with wisdom. He was only fourteen years older than me, but those few years seemed like decades to a boy still in school, and he wore that black-and-white collar, and his eyes could burn me like sunlight through a magnifying glass. I used to think about when I turned sixty-four, Father Brown would be seventy-eight, and I guessed we would have made it to even ground, and be more like good friends.

Father Brown and the captain talked long into lots of nights and shared good Scotch whisky many times. Though my father said that if "the priest" set up the drinks it was not the good stuff, and I heard Father Brown remind him of a priest's wage when he complained.

When Father Brown showed up on Fly Creek, he stood on the bank and called out, in a sailor's best etiquette, "Ahoy, *Sea Bird!* Permission to come aboard."

I was belowdecks, straightening up the cabin, getting ready for his visit, not expecting him so soon. I popped my head up through the open hatch, standing on the lower step of the companionway ladder. His seamanlike greeting made me feel more like a sailor than I ever had, and I was grinning like the Cheshire cat, so wide and full of teeth that I, too, might have disappeared behind my smile like Alice's feline friend.

"Permission granted. Come aboard." I gave a quick look around the cabin, found everything in place, and went up the ladder and into the cockpit. I extended a hand to the priest as he tugged the sloop near the bank with the stern line and stepped onto the deck. He was barefoot.

"She looks good, Rove. You've done a superb job of sprucing up the old gal." Father Brown looked the sloop over, moving underneath the boom and going forward until he stood on the short foredeck, his hand gripping the forestay for balance. I sat in the cockpit, my hand on the tiller.

"Does the cabin roof leak at all?" he asked.

"No, I recaulked a couple of spots and replaced a section of canvas. After three coats of good paint, she's tight against the elements," I said.

"That's good. You'll have plenty of *elements* before this

night is over, I think." The priest let his eyes follow the stays and shrouds, scrutinized the halyards. "Looks like you've got a little slop in your standing rigging." He kept looking up. "The main halyard's frayed some in the block at the top of the mast."

"Those items are next on my list. Anna Pearl told me at school she's going to give me a hand with that work." And Father Brown agreed that she could get the job done. "Your father can help, too," he added.

"The way he's been acting lately, I don't want him around my boat," I said, realizing in afterthought that Father Brown would have no reference for what I'd just said. But, nonetheless, I was not prepared for the rapid change in the priest's demeanor.

"Now, see here, Rove. I've known your father since my first week at Holy Family, and I can tell you that Germany's attack on Poland two years ago had the effect of an attack on his own mind." Father Brown's pontifical air was intimidating, but I didn't look away from him. "Rove, I know you, like anyone else in this country with eyes to see and ears to hear, must be appalled and outraged by the behavior of these Germans," said the priest, becoming more agitated and animated.

"But an attack on sleeping American sailors last week," he continued, "is a horror to the soul, and an affront to my religion. I know as soon as Captain MacNee makes his first port of call and gets the news, he will turn that schooner around and come home."

"I expect you're right, Father. I don't know what he can do, though."

"What do you mean? What can any of us do here at home but whatever we can to support the cause of defeating these treacherous Japanese, and Hitler."

The priest's words identified our enemies, one as a country and the other as a man. Father Brown charged on. "President Roosevelt's signature on the declaration of war will alter the course of this country's future. We have joined much of the rest of the world in a bloody years' long war—who knows how long? Who knows how each citizen will be called upon to assist?"

I sat dazed by the priest's angry homily, which seemed to me, somehow, to settle something of the war on my shoulders, and the weight of the realization was breaking something in me.

"Your father came to the church. He asked me to—" Father Brown hesitated. "Captain MacNee believes that even ships of commerce will become the targets of German U-boats, that smoke from the flames of piracy will darken the horizon on American waters."

"Father Brown," I had to interrupt him, "what does this war have to do with me on this boat?"

"Hellfire! Rove, who can know? Your father may have a point with Josef Unruh. I cannot swear that he's not providing information to submarines in the Gulf, out there in this very bay."

Father Brown plowed on with evangelical fervor. "My

own church ignores the stories seeping back from the cesspool of Hitler's ruthless and rapacious Nazi regime. But, there are men who will not sit still. Men like your father will not commit the sin of complicity in silence and inaction."

"So he will—what, Father?—mount guns on the deck of the *Mary Foster?* And blow away Josef Unruh's windmill?"

"Rove MacNee, I find your impudence unbecoming. And I believe you should be less accusatory of your father."

I told the priest that I judged only what I saw, and that I'd seen him assault a man with his hunting knife. Pretty simple, I told him. He looked at me, and the longer he gazed at me, the more his face relaxed and his eyes softened.

Father Brown sighed, saying, "I wish it were simple, Rove. But you and I both know it is not even close to simple."

The truth of his statement was underscored by the silence that fell on the two of us, and we sat briefly in the cockpit without speaking a word to each other. Then he said he had an appointment with a parishioner. Easy as that, my shoulder was leaving. But worse, he added: "Are you absolutely sure about this move to the creek, Rove?"

I answered quickly and too loudly, "No. Of course, I'm not sure! But are you sure about the outcome of your day's doings, Father?"

"I'm sorry, Rove. I know you have much on your mind.

It gives me comfort, my faith in you, in your mind, to handle the trouble of these days better than most." With that Father Brown stepped off the *Sea Bird*. He turned around and waved from the top of the rise. When he was gone from view, the silence of the trees and the creek rang in my head, and the image of Josef Unruh the sailor swam before my eyes.

Between the excitement of camping the first night on my sloop in Fly Creek, the exchange with Father Brown, and a storm that had come stomping around in the middle of the night, I had spent a rather fitful night. I awakened tired.

It seemed the last several days had been characterized by nights that dragged on with a double handful of trouble stirring in my mind and keeping me twisted in my sheets, flopping on my bed like a mullet on the beach. If what lay ahead could be written on the smooth slate of late afternoon sky, it would be dappled like the mackerel sky that tells a sailor the weather will break down soon. With such knowledge and anticipation, there was tension that pulled at the muscles in my neck and shoulders.

The cold front that trundled through during the middle of the night, as Father Brown had predicted it would, clashed with yesterday's warm air and the night had lit up with lightning and rolled with thunder. Before dawn I had been awakened in my forward vee-berth by a sudden rain making a racket on the roof of the *Sea Bird* like a bandit in the night intent on stopping the heart of the sleeping one he'd come to drag off.

I had come full awake this morning with the first rain striking the roof of the boat and sat straight up wondering, as I nearly always did when surprised by a deluge at Magnolia Bayhouse, if the windows were up on the Buick. It was an automatic response, and when the fog of sleep cleared and I remembered where I was, that I was on Fly Creek aboard my boat, and I had in fact put up the windows on the Buick when Julian and I returned it to Magnolia Bayhouse, I relaxed. But I was now fully awake and decided to make some coffee.

I had once sat in the family car playing at driving—I might have been seven—turning the big ivory-looking steering wheel left and right and making engine sounds and seeing worlds rise up in front of the windshield. When later I went inside the house, I left the windows rolled down on the car.

In the morning the captain had gone out to get into the automobile and discovered two inches of water standing on the floorboards and the mohair seats soaked through. My father woke me and told me his car was flooded inside, then gave me a spanking. Now coming awake to the sound of a heavy downpour almost always caused my heart to bang in panic.

Then I rolled off my berth and padded to the little

stove in the galley. I thought of the hatch in the cockpit. I'd had it off last night after Father Brown left, and I wondered if I'd secured it properly. I went through the cabin aft to the companionway ladder. Standing on the first step, I peeked through cracks between the pinboards and saw through the pouring rain the hatch cover in place.

I was anxious about my boat, and knew there were details of the overhaul that I'd not yet checked off the list. The frayed rigging in the upper shrouds now caught my eye like a yellow flag. The groan from the rudder's pintles and gudgeons meant a weakened fastening that could break under stress and cause the loss of steerage. The repairs could be made safely in port. Even without clear bearings on my course ahead, I would have to simply be ready. I'd start on the work today.

But at the moment it was still dark outside on the creek. The rocking motion of the boat increased, the main and jib halyards slapped against the mast, *thack-thack, thack-thack,* marking time for the music of the wind as it blew harder down the creek.

I started a fire on my kerosene-stove burner. I had never drunk much coffee at home, but it seemed the right way for a sailor to start his morning, so I'd have a pot of coffee. I filled the aluminum pot with water and spooned some coffee grounds into the top, and put it all back together with the little tube up the middle of the filter basket. I pumped up the pressure on the kerosene reservoir and put a match to the stove top, switched on the valve, and a blue-yellow flame popped up in a circle around the burner. I reached overhead and slid the hatch back a crack to ventilate the cabin.

When the coffee was ready, I boiled water and made some grits for my breakfast. My mother had wrapped some cold biscuits in waxed paper and put them into my basket. It suddenly dawned on me that I would not be able to bake bread on the *Sea Bird,* and I wondered how long I could keep a sourdough loaf. I had some research to do. Maybe I'd go back and read again about the voyage of the *Spray,* this time taking careful notes on things like provisioning a boat instead of daydreaming.

The main salon grew warm quickly, and I opened the companionway hatch entirely, removed the pinboards, and stowed them in the rack made to hold them overhead above the quarter berth. The coffee smelled great in the boat. I went forward and tugged on my trousers and shirt and boots, stretched tight and tucked in the bedding on my vee-berth, and went back to the tiny galley area on the sloop and poured myself another cup of coffee.

At home I would have gone for the sugar and some milk, but I figured I might as well learn to stick to the very basics with my food rations, and decided I'd train myself to drink black coffee. It was steaming hot, and I set the cup on the counter and quickly stowed some things my mother had put together into a basket for me from her pantry: a three-pound bag of white rice, a jar of honey, a tin of coffee, a box of powdered milk, some dried beans.

I retrieved my coffee and balanced it as I stepped up

the ladder and out of the cabin and stood in the cockpit. God, how I loved this view: the creek bending away past either end of my boat, the grasses and mosses and wild shrubs at the water's edge, the trees on the banks that climbed gently upward from the creek toward the high ground. I draped my left arm over the boom, with the mainsail bunched there underneath a faded blue canvas cover.

It had stopped raining, but puffy clouds hung low and dirty, and I decided I would take the skiff and row out to the mouth of the creek and look around. I finished my coffee, rinsed the cup, and stowed it belowdecks. I went back topside, checked the mooring lines, and stepped ashore.

Up the creek bank a few steps, upside down and tied off to a tree, was a thirteen-foot flat-bottom skiff. I dragged the boat down to the creek and shoved it in and went back for the oars, where they were leaned against a tree. It was cold, and I turned up my collar before easing into the skiff and taking up the rowing.

The small boat moved easily and ghosted along around the bends in the creek. The little splashing dip and lift of the oars was the only sound until I arrived in the curve of Fly Creek where it widened into a backwater harbor and bent ninety degrees west, running maybe another hundred yards to Mobile Bay. A dozen or so fishing boats were moored here, a motley collection of trawler-style high-bowed, broad-beamed vessels with narrow curved wheelhouses and substantial stems to part the sea, thick-planked boats made for fishing and heavy weather. The fishermen's catch was off-loaded into an icehouse attached to a small store with a tin roof and block walls painted white, no windows, only a broad, rolling door that stood perennially open. FRESH FISH—SHRIMP—CRABS was crudely painted in big black letters on the side of the store.

I heard my name called and shipped the oars while turning my head to see Anna Pearl and another girl at the fish market docks. The other girl, whom I did not recognize, was paying the man at the weighing scales for a few pounds of fish wrapped in brown paper. Anna Pearl said something to her friend and ran toward the seawall, and I steered my boat over.

"I cannot believe you did it, Rove! You really did it. I saw Father Brown at early mass and he said he'd sat aboard the *Sea Bird* with you last night."

"Hi, Anna Pearl," I said, holding the boat steady with a hand on a piling near the seawall. "Father Brown? Why're you going to mass in the middle of the week?"

"Oh, Mother insisted since I won't be here on Sunday morning. I'm going over to Mobile with my friend Sally when she and her mother go home on Friday. But never mind that. Tell me what you are doing! Do I still get to help some on the boat?"

"Sure, I don't imagine I'll be finished by the time you get back. You see I'm taking it kind of easy."

"I do see that, and I'm coming home Sunday night." Anna Pearl looked over her shoulder to check on her friend, who had finished her purchase and was walking with her package toward a light green Ford sedan.

"Sally," she called out, but the girl kept walking. "Do you mind waiting just a moment, Rove? Let me—well, I'll be right back." And without waiting to see what I had to say, she darted off in the direction of her friend at the car. Anna Pearl's dress was billowing out and flying up around her knees as she ran. Her hair was bouncing on her shoulders, and I did not take my eyes off her.

In two minutes she came walking back, smiling, her eyes filled with purpose.

"Will you let me go with you? Sally doesn't like it at all," Anna Pearl said with a little huff, "but she consented to driving around to the park by the Big Pier to pick me up in forty-five minutes. Can you row that far that fast?" She tossed out the small challenge with a twinkle of mischief in her eyes.

"I can row down there easy," I said, my voice firm. "If I can't, I'll rest in the bow and let you row. How's that?"

"You've got a deal, Captain."

"Will you be warm enough? That's a thin coat."

"I will be warm as toast. Just help me aboard, and we'll shove off then."

I stood up in the skiff and, hanging on to the piling, pushed the bow over to the seawall and held it there while Anna Pearl bunched up her dress in her hand and stepped daintily onto the narrow foredeck, then bent over and held onto the gunwale as she negotiated herself to the next seat and sat down facing aft. I sat down facing forward this time, and lifted the oars over the side and rowed surely out to the middle of the creek. Some of the fishermen were making catcalls, which embarrassed me, but I said nothing. Then, "Are you all right, Anna Pearl?"

"Peachy. I know you're good in a boat." She kept her eyes on me, then looked toward the beach south, in the direction we were going. "Sally is so mad at me. But I don't think she will tell Mother. We'll still be home by the time lunch is on the table."

"You'll eat your fish raw then?" I grinned.

"Of course, silly. Don't you?" She rolled her eyes. "No, the fish is for supper. Would you like to come?"

"Is that so Sally will never speak to you again?"

"No. So she can see that you are not a smelly wharf rat. Please."

"I don't think so, but thank you just the same."

I grew serious, and Anna Pearl noted this and said nothing else as we approached the breakwater at the mouth of the creek. I studied the bay, satisfied that I had only a very slight chop to deal with, and with the high sides on this fishing skiff, my passenger would not get soaked with spray, which, for some reason, I did not imagine she would be greatly bothered by. It would be an easy row for me. The overcast had lifted some and lost its rolling texture, and was now gone to a smooth galvanized hue. The wind lay down within yards and the water settled quickly, and I knew it would soon be as slick as the sky overhead.

I would have liked to say something, but without the benefit of some clever retort to something Anna Pearl said, which I found much easier than straightforward conversation with this beautiful girl, I said nothing. Anna Pearl sat seemingly transfixed by the view of the water and the tree-lined beach seventy-five yards off to her right and the air in her face as the skiff moved easily ahead of my oar strokes.

While Anna Pearl looked at the beach, I looked at her. The soft, muted light under the gray sky had the effect of surrounding her with a warm silvered reflection off the water, and her face was rosy and her hair was shining and her eyes looked lost in a waking dream. When she looked at me, caught me staring at her, she only looked away, and the corners of her mouth rose in a sweet little-girl smile that did not seem put on for my attention.

As I dipped the oars and pulled deeply into the green water, I noticed an approaching trio of brown pelicans. They sailed along on gliding wings scant inches above their verdigris reflections. I tucked my chin into my collar. Anna Pearl lifted the wide collar on her coat, but sat straight-backed and otherwise looked to me oblivious to the damp cold air. A great blue heron flew in toward the beach, angling from the southwest and on a direct track toward the pelicans. The lanky giant gronked loudly twice, fussing at the pelicans who gave me no quarter.

"Look," I said, and nodded toward the other fliers, who'd given up fishing for the day it seemed, heading for rest onshore. There was not a quack from the half dozen mallards or a whistle from the slickered loon as we held to a flight plan that brought them very near the skiff as it went also toward the beach a little ways south of the mouth of Fly Creek. A little breeze had freshened from the north and gave the boat a boost in speed. Anna Pearl was smiling fully now and said to me, "This is delicious. You are so generous."

I nodded and returned her smile. I could see the green Ford parked between two big junipers, the driver still at the wheel. I pulled hard once, twice, three times on the oars, and the boat surged ahead and its bow slid up on the low slope of brown sand.

"Are you coming ashore, Rove?"

"No, I'd better get on back to the creek ahead of the chop that'll soon build in front of this wind coming up."

"Then stay put," she said, standing and turning to step off the bow. Anna Pearl hopped onto the beach and turned and put both hands on the bow and gave it a strong push with a small *ummph*. She stood up straight and waved to me as the skiff slid back out into the waves. "Thank you, Rove MacNee," she said, her hand still in the air. "I've never had a better boat ride in my life."

I turned in my seat, now facing aft, and worked the oars and brought the skiff about with a graceful motion and was heading back out into the bay. I stopped rowing, sat up straight, and called, "I'll see you in the creek sometime." I could not, and did not, try to disguise my hopefulness.

By the time I came in sight of the *Sea Bird,* the wind

was stirring again and had bunched up the clouds into pillows of gray-black. Distant thunder rolled across the delta fifteen miles to the north. I was surprised by the deterioration of the weather so soon behind last night's front. Ordinarily I would have expected sunshine, or partly cloudy skies, but now it looked like it might turn out cold and gray. If it did, there'd be a light drizzle peppering the creek, and one of those gloomy weather patterns that looks like it will hold until the stars fall.

That is precisely what happened.

So I got no work done on the *Sea Bird*'s rigging, didn't even look at the rudder or the sails, and opted to stay below in the warm cabin and read and write in my logbook.

"My spirit forms different ideas in my head," I penciled, "here on this boat, moored in this winding creek. I sit in the cockpit and let the wind blow damp and chilly and brush my cheek and I know it's kicking up whitecaps out on the bay, making music in the cypresses over on the beach, rattling its way through the masts and halyards of the sailboats tied up along Fly Creek, moaning in the rigging of the working boats at the fishing docks, and I hear the whistling, percussive symphony and it is a different melody from the cacophonous gale curling around Magnolia Bayhouse. I go below and before sliding the hatch closed, give a last listen. It's my song they're playing, and this is a good place to call home."

Old Jenny, as the Organic School service truck was known, was a 1933 Chevy stake-bed truck that had spent its first five years picking up and delivering McKean's Hardware store orders. Kate Anderson's brother Wesley then bought it and put it into service for his Ingle's Dry Goods store, and two years later, when Anna Pearl's mother had become headmistress at Organic, he gave it to her for use at the school.

Anna Pearl kept the truck's dark green paint and black fenders and running boards shining and often took it home at the end of the school day, returning it the next morning to Fred the maintenance man. Fred might use the truck to haul in lunchroom supplies from Nelson's grocery store; he might go into town to bring in a donated desk or some boxes of books; he might move chairs from a classroom to the assembly hall.

Often as not, though, Old Jenny was stripped of her stake side panels and its flatbed was a transport for students to and from this and that field trip, driven at low speeds to minimize injuries to the occasional child who was bounced from his seat and onto the road or the shoulder of the road. If admonitions were issued in such cases, it was almost never to the school for negligence; rather the inattentive and careless student would be cuffed for interrupting the field trip with a banged elbow or scraped knee.

When the muffler had fallen off the truck at the outset of this term, Fred had welded in its place a section of straight pipe, and the voice of the truck dropped like an adolescent boy's at thirteen. In fact, it quite bellowed under acceleration, and Anna Pearl did not creep about when she drove Old Jenny down Section Street to the meadows south of town or west out Fairhope Avenue toward the farmers' potato sheds. Her mother had received complaints about the noise and the speed of the vehicle from more than one person in her lovely home along Mobile Street, where it paralleled the bay on its jog south toward the Grand Hotel at Point Clear, a scenic six-mile ride that Anna Pearl told me was her favorite stretch for motoring.

I heard her coming in the truck for a half mile before she reached the shell drive that wound through the woods from Section Street down to Fly Creek. The road was rutted and partly grown over with tall grasses and brush that scratched with knobby branches at the sides of the truck. The narrow lane angled in off the street at a point a few hundred yards north of where my footpath turned toward the creek, so I didn't really know the rough ride Anna Pearl was getting on her way to help me work on the *Sea Bird*. I learned firsthand, however, when later my teeth were rattled in the passenger seat as the two of us jostled along proceeding out of the woods with my boat's boom lashed to the bed of the truck.

Anna Pearl was taking me and my cracked boom to a boatbuilder on the causeway, a gifted craftsman, Carlton Smith, who worked with wood the way a poet works with words, joining oak to mahogany like the right strong verb is married to its subject for the surest meaning, the deepest rapport between the poet and his reader.

I had discovered a hairline crack in the fir spar just behind the bronze coupling where it was shackled to the mast. Anna Pearl and I had removed the mainsail so she could restitch some seams and reinforce the tack and the clew, and that's when I spied a tiny dark line in the grain. Maybe it was nothing, but I wanted another opinion. I had seen four of the boats that Carlton Smith had built, a rowing skiff, a small sailing dory, and two motorboats, and the workmanship was fine. My father had shown me the first one, had told me about the slow and sure methods adhered to in the Smith boat shop, how each piece of wood was selected for the right grain and how the joinery employed was equal to the best furniture made. Glue at the seams was not allowed to drip and run; fasteners were aligned and evenly spaced. I could trust this man's advice on the cracked boom.

I spoke above the jarring and squeaking of the truck as we bounced up the wooded lane toward the street. "I do appreciate your help, Anna Pearl. You know that if Father Brown sees us together, you helping me out on the boat, I mean," I said, "he'd surely get your mother down here, and you'd be forbidden to sew another single stitch. You'd probably be banned from driving Old Jenny, too."

"Oh, the priest has already spoken to Mother. She came to me and we talked yesterday," Anna Pearl said, turning the big steering wheel to avoid a washout in the road. She downshifted to second gear. "I told her that it was entirely your business and privilege to decide to live on your own. It would be between you and your father and mother if they don't want you to stay on your boat."

"And what did Miss Anderson say to that?" I asked.

"She agreed completely."

"It's a good thing my father's not here," I added. "I think he would lead a squad of men against Mr. Unruh. I almost wish Mr. Unruh would leave town until—"

"Until when?" Anna Pearl interrupted. "I think we're in for a long wait, Rove." She braked the truck as we neared the street, rolling up to the pavement at Section Street. There were no other automobiles in sight, and she swung onto the street, heading north. "I just don't think it's possible to manage all the million contingencies." She reached past the floor shifter and patted my knee. "I, for one, think you're doing the right thing. You know, just creating a little distance for yourself."

"That was kind of my plan. Let the bombs hit—" I stopped, considered my choice of words, and said, "I don't intend disrespect, it just works." Then I told Anna Pearl that it seemed sensible to then let some of the smoke clear and try to make a reasonable response. She agreed that there was, in truth, not much else I could do.

We continued north and would drive twenty minutes to Spanish Fort and find the boat shop at the foot of the hill, tucked away in the shadow of the bluff right on the edge of the Blakeley River. It was one of five rivers feeding the delta system at the north end of Mobile Bay—the Appalachee, the Tensaw, the Spanish, and the Mobile were the other four fanning east to west, with Chocalata Bay and Polecat Bay holding their backwaters.

"This is pretty up here at this end of the bay," Anna Pearl said. "I like the way the land just bucks up, like it's lifting its head and shoulder as though it's got something to see down that way." She hooked her left thumb toward the window at her shoulder and to the silver waters of the bay spreading behind us to the south. The noonday sun scattered a sparkle across the water, and you could see the wind moving there like dark strokes from a painter's broad brush. Anna Pearl downshifted to let the engine slow our descent down the hill. The six-cylinder motor whined.

"It's a small place, a shed, really. Mr. Smith works by himself," I said. "I was here only once with my father. I hope we find him at work in his shop today."

"Do you have any money, Rove?" Anna Pearl asked, not following my comments. I was surprised at the question, and then thought to myself, how like a woman to be so practical.

"I've got three hundred and fifty dollars," I said. "It's money that my grandmother gave to me a little here and a little there over several years, including some that I earned crewing for my father."

"He paid you? His own son?"

"His own rules. My father said he would accept no indentured servitude as a condition of work on his boat. 'A man works, a man is paid.' That's what he said. So I earned what a green sailor would have made."

"What do you think will happen when he comes home this time?"

"That he will motor up to Magnolia Bayhouse in his skiff, rush up the beach and embrace his loving elder son, cuff my brother good-naturedly on the shoulder, and kiss my mother while winking at his children over her shoulder. Then we'll sit down to a homecoming repast fit for a captain of the high seas and his faithful family, and sit together after in the parlor and talk about good books—"

Whatever other of my foolish make-believe I might have woven for Anna Pearl was taken right off my tongue when she took both hands off the steering wheel and, hardly slowing at all, took the back of my head in her hands and drew my face quickly to the center of the cab and kissed me full on my mouth. When she let me go, my head was spinning and my lips tingled and continued to feel the sweet phantom pain of that moment as if she still had her mouth on mine.

"Anna Pearl, what are you doing?" I could not think of a single thing to say in response to the girl's impulsive affection that made any sense to me at all. "You'll kill us driving like that," was what came from me, my cheeks flushed and warm, my eyes locked on nothing out beyond the windscreen, my brain electrified.

Anna Pearl pushed her fingers through her hair, shifted the truck into high gear, and eased the speed up slightly. There was a turn to the right up ahead, away from the river, and a widening of the road into something of a parking place, though whatever establishment it approached could not be seen around the motley stand of junipers. Anna Pearl patted my knee again. "And you will die with a smile on your lips, sailor boy."

When Carlton Smith had done with the boom, we lashed it to the oak planking of the Chevy truck's bed, and Anna Pearl motored south back toward Fairhope. The highway was in good shape if a little wavy on some stretches, but there were no potholes. I watched Anna Pearl push the speed up past forty miles an hour. The windows were rolled down, the air outside was comfortable, warm for December.

I stared ahead. Anna Pearl concentrated on the road in front of the truck. When I looked over at her, careful not to turn my head, moving only my eyes, she sat with her hands on the wheel, the wind tossing her hair into shiny curls and loops. Her cheeks were smooth and looked to me soft as a kitten's ear. She really kissed me. Not a sisterly peck, a warm and damp kiss. And now she was going down the blacktop highway double-clutching a flatbed Chevy, and, maybe, for her, miles past the moment. The aftereffect on me, however, had settled in my solar plexus like a kick, and my breathing wouldn't go as deep as it should.

The truck bounced over a bump in the road, jarring me back to the small cab and the wind down my collar and the rev of the engine and the Fairhope city limits sign.

"Look at the sky," Anna Pearl said, nodding toward the west out my window. The short day had almost gone, and through the trees over toward the horizon along the Mobile side of the bay, a ragged carpet of high, thin clouds was tinged with yellow light. But the colors were changing more quickly than I remembered ever seeing before. It was almost like the first light was a spark that caught the sky afire, and now a furious gold and burning orange light from the sun ripped across the bay where the two of us could see it through a break in the tree line, setting ablaze everything in its path. Nothing was spared. Least of all the wispy cotton sky.

Anna Pearl had slowed the truck, she and I both mesmerized by the swirl of colors growing from the western sky like flames licking ever higher. The silhouetted tree line between us and the bay indeed seemed to be shielding us from a horrible forest fire. At the next clearing in the trees, at a long, lazy dip in the street, we could see down to the bay again. I began to shake my head. Anna Pearl mumbled, "Would you look at that." We immediately agreed to drive on past the lane down to Fly Creek, where *Sea Bird* was tied up, and go down to the Big Pier for a better look.

When we arrived, Anna Pearl and I discovered several others had the same idea. People were stepping out of automobiles, walking down the hill toward the city pier, coming out of doors, and turning up their collars as the wind came up quick and biting, stiff and fresh out of the north. All looked mindless of the cold and lost in enchantment. One might guess the people were gathering in reverence to witness an approaching flyover by a squadron of American fighter planes.

But it was just a sunset, such as happens every day. But not every day, I knew, with the terrible beauty of that day. The western sky was an arcing crescent of brilliance from north toward the Mobile delta down to Bayou La Batre, gathering the mind like an insight in the midst of confusion. I stood beside Anna Pearl on the bluff. I tapped her shoulder and pointed out the black outline of a freighter that had moved into the southern end of the bay. The northerly was sweeping the air clean and you could see plainly the rumpled tree line across on the other shore, usually no more than a hazy dark stain above the water.

On this day it seemed you could make out the silhouette of individual trees.

A man stood bent over behind a big camera on a tripod, the barrel of the black box pointing straight toward the setting sun, and I wondered what kind of picture the man would get. I knew nothing about photography. Granny Wooten had said once on the gallery of Magnolia Bayhouse at sundown that an artist can't paint a sunset and shouldn't even try. Then she'd said, and I could hear her voice still, "Reincarnated expressly for the purpose, Mozart and Van Gogh and Shakespeare all rolled into one couldn't handle the task of expressing a magnificent sunset."

Then she'd told me that Cervantes's Don Quixote took a stab at it. "Remember?" She asked me the question as though it would have been something I'd read within the last several days. She raised her voice and quoted with the animation of an actor, "The rubicund Apollo spread over the face of the broad and spacious earth the gilded filaments of his beauteous locks."

She raised her arms, and I had been a bit embarrassed even though it was only the two of us on the porch. "O wise magician to whom shall fall the task of chronicling this extraordinary sunset, this turning of the world to show the sun's face as never before."

I knew better now than then that not even a magician with words or paints or music could handle the picture in the sky when God is feeling frisky, showing off, baking for his mortal children the daily bread of the eye.

I guessed that was why, when the evening sky had chased the sun's last rays below the western horizon, Anna Pearl made the trip back to the boat in silence. Like the mystic's comprehension of reality, we'd seen it and realized there was not much to be said about it. Like a boy's first kiss from a pretty girl, some things are just for the having, not for the telling.

Anna Pearl came to help me resew some seams on the *Sea Bird*'s main and jib. She showed up with her mother's sewing kit and a few spools of cotton thread.

"You can't use household needles and thread on sails," I laughed.

"You laugh at me again and you'll be looking for other slave labor, Rove MacNee," Anna Pearl said. If I hadn't been in the line of fire of her scowl, I could have assumed she meant to be funny.

I apologized and showed her the fat needles and heavy waxed thread she'd need to use for reinforcing the tack and clew, the tips of the triangle that is a sail, where grommets are sewn in for hauling up and holding down and stretching out the canvas into a nice airfoil shape when under sail. There's incredible tension at these points, and the stitching there must be strong and reliable.

Anna Pearl gave a little *hmmph* and a roll of her eyes and was about to fall right to work. I told her she would need to use the leather sewing palm, and this time she asked me what that was without bristling, though she didn't look at me when she spoke.

I took the piece of worn leather strap from the tool kit, showed her how her thumb fit through the hole in the strap and the rest of it wrapped around her palm, that the buttonlike disc on the strap was for pushing the sharp awl through layers of canvas.

"Let me have it then," she said, still a bit miffed with me. I was about to give her a small lesson in the use of the sewing palm, but she put it right on and used it reasonably well. Her fingers moved deftly and with skill.

"Well, you're a quick study with the sewing palm and awl," I said, probably overcompensating. When she cut her eyes toward me, breaking her concentration for a second, she poked the awl into her thumb deeply enough to draw lots of blood and mansized profanity.

"Damn it!" And as the blood flowed over her palm, "Oh, that hurts like hell," she said. I pulled a clean handkerchief from my pocket and reached to take her hand, but she snatched it back. She flipped over the sailcloth so it wouldn't get blood on it and quickly removed the leather sewing palm.

"A lot of good that thing is," she said with a pout, sticking her bleeding thumb into her mouth.

"Okay," I said, "enough work for today."

"I didn't lose a limb, Rove."

"I know," I said, tossing her the white handkerchief. "Press that against the blood flow. But I was thinking anyway that I'd like to walk down to the bay with my cast net and see if there are some mullet who want badly to be my supper. Do you want to go with me?"

"No. You know, I think I'll go home," she said. "My mother mentioned walking with her to town this afternoon. She wanted to get a few things at Nelson's store. I'll go and help her carry the groceries home."

Anna Pearl stood up, clutching the cloth into her palm. I was still seated in the cockpit, and she bent forward and gave me a light kiss on my forehead. For some reason, I'd been sure she'd go with me to the beach. I didn't conceal my disappointment well, because she gave me a pat on the head and said, "It'll feel good for you to take a walk in the sunshine, alone, Rove. You've got some things to sort out. I'll come back tomorrow, or the next day, and we'll finish the few things on your list. Then you will only have left to decide when you'll set sail."

"You don't have to come back, Anna Pearl. I can finish what's left to do."

"You don't have to get your feelings hurt, Rove," she said. "But those smoky eyes do add a handsome flair to your good looks."

I blushed at that. She might have smiled, I don't know. I didn't look at her. And she did me the courtesy to drop the matter, and stepped off the *Sea Bird,* calling out to me that she would see me soon, over her shoulder, as she went up the knoll to where her truck was parked.

I sat a minute after the truck's loud exhaust had followed her out of the woods, and the creek was quiet. The silence was sweet. No birds twittered or animals chattered, and the only sound was a low gurgle from the creek that was easy to let slip from consciousness.

Some things to sort out.

I'd done such a good job, too, pretending that I was a boy on a boat with not a care in the world. But I could feel the events of the last few days tugging downward at the flesh on my face. When I smiled, or laughed, as I did at Anna Pearl, the mood flew away quickly, like a puff of smoke from the captain's pipe on a blustery day. Anna Pearl was right. I just needed to take a walk. Maybe throw my net down at the bay, even though I now had no appetite at all for fish I might catch.

Some things to sort out.

The captain was home. He'd sent word this morning by Father Brown that I was to be at Magnolia Bayhouse before sunset. I was not surprised that my father had sailed back so quickly. Father Brown had probably been right on the button when he suggested that the *Mary Foster* would virtually spin on her keel turning for home when the captain got the news of the Japanese bombing. The country was now at war, and the thick of things is where Dominus MacNee would rather be, and if he were a younger man, or if the navy would take a man his age, he'd be shipping out tomorrow. Short of that, he would set up a home guard, himself in command, and keep his sights on Josef Unruh. There was no other target, really, except for a giant figmental force whose clandestine operations were being carried out within arm's reach. It was only a matter of time until the rough beast would come marching down Section Street. And the whole town, it seemed, was at the ready for its arrival.

Fellows I'd known in school, who had graduated in the last two or so years, were enlisting to fight the enemy, *the krauts and the slant-eyes*. Younger boys were marching with their BB guns and taping on wooden bayonets. Veterans of the Great War, home for more than twenty years, were fighting again at the barbershop and the soda fountain.

And on the other hand, the town's rumor mill was all abuzz with talk about how some of the Quaker menfolk were talking openly of gathering their families and setting off to start a colony somewhere else. The Fairhope Religious Society of Friends, the Quakers, had quite a large membership, and it was known, generally, that they were opposed to war.

But, from the backyard fences to the loafer's bench at the hardware store to the corner sidewalk by the Ford dealership, all agreed that bombing our sailors in their sleep defined the sentiment behind an eye for an eye. To everything, according to the Holy Bible itself, there is a season, and this was the time to take up swords. This was the season for war.

But the Quakers did not see it that way, and within ten years, in 1951, in protest of the draft, almost four dozen of the Fairhope Friends would leave town and go together to Costa Rica, where they would buy a mountain and found a village called Monte Verde that would thrive in peaceful solitude, with monkeys making faces and scratching their bellies for the tourists who would come to the quaint Quaker hotel and sit in wicker chairs on the gallery and ruminate on their busy lives back in the States.

Some things to sort out.

Anna Pearl and I had stood outside the truck after returning from the boat shop in Spanish Fort, after witnessing God's own sunset, and we were coiling the lines we'd used to secure the mast to the truck bed for its transport home. Something was bothering Anna Pearl. I even guessed she had something she wanted to say to me, but was skirting nervously around it.

When she finally said, "Rove," in that way that let me know she'd decided to speak her mind, her green eyes went to a shadowy jade and conveyed her determination to get it said, the thing on her mind.

"When I went by your house to get your satchel of books like you asked, well," she looked away toward the river. "Josef Unruh was there. I went inside without knocking and surprised your mother and him sitting close together on the settee in the parlor. He was holding your mother's hand. I'm not sure that it means anything, but—"

"What did she say to you?" I demanded.

"Just, 'Anna Pearl.' She didn't have time to say more. I said excuse me and bolted from the house."

Some things to sort out.

I was not a boy on a boat. I was hobbled with confusion and uncertainty, a kind of aggravated adolescent malaise worse for the unsortable fallout from Anna Pearl's bomb.

She held my hand and said she was sorry, but that she believed it was right for me to know.

"Know *what*? Can you tell me what it is that I know?"

"Are you angry with me?" she wanted to know, and let go of my hand. "I troubled over telling you, Rove. But I was afraid your mother would bring it up, would say something about what I saw. Then if I had said nothing—well . . ."

Anna Pearl said it was a mess, and was still herself upset when she said good-bye. I asked her to come back, and she promised to visit tomorrow afternoon. By the time I got my bucket and net, the wind had turned to the north and was freshening, but not yet causing a big blow. I decided on a sweater, and when I reached the beach below the mouth of Fly Creek, I was glad for the heavier sleeve. It would keep me warm enough on my stroll along the beach. There was a finger pier not far south, and I'd take up a watchful post out on it and wait for a school of mullet.

Turns out, I just kept walking, swinging my bucket, being spun around in my stride by my thoughts, swinging my bucket. *Nothing getting sorted out.*

I walked for an hour, sat for two, walked some more, and finally turned and headed back in the direction I'd come. Twilight was approaching. My net was still coiled and dry in the bucket. My nose was not even pointed in the direction of my father's house. And it was not the captain I did not want to see.

I was walking on the sand near the water's edge, watching the sun settle across the water on the horizon at Dog River, like a glowing red balloon above Mobile Bay. The beach is a good spot for spending that transitional hour between day and night as the waves roll up and slide back, tugging out some of a busy day's wrinkles.

That day, in the soft orange glow, I saw as I walked a movement on the edge of my vision to the right, higher up on the beach. At first I thought it was a seagull, but this fellow sported a longer orange beak and a tuft of feathers on the back of his head. He was a royal tern. I could tell something was wrong with the bird. His black eyes, when I'd got close enough to see well, were dry and dull like coal. Spreading his wings in a takeoff gesture, he stumbled forward onto his fat, round chest. He staggered up then and stood still and watched me. The tern waited to see if I meant to bother him.

I stood still and watched him.

We watched each other.

I wondered what was wrong with the tern as it stood there wobbling like one of the wine-sopped sailors I'd seen come back aboard my father's *Mary Foster* in New Orleans after a night of liberty, hardly fit to man a vessel on a 150-mile trip back home.

The tern seemed fit to do nothing, and I wondered at its predicament. My mind went first to some kind of meanness. A few weeks back some mallards from the ponds along a stretch of beach south of here had died mysteriously, and everyone suspected poisoning. Though no one had a good theory for the means or the why, I wondered if the tern was a similar victim. Maybe some farm chemical had spilled and polluted a creek or pond, or rat poison had gotten into some feed corn.

It seemed an awfully complicated scenario, so as I watched, I began to doubt such intrigue. What I knew was that I was looking at a sick bird. Its behavior reminded me of a doddering old person, and I went with that thought for a while, a little surprised that the bird might be simply dying of old age. I'd never really stopped to think about animals getting old, that their winged machine at some point would fail them and they would not be able to catch food, or rise up in flight, and they would die. I had not ever put the picture in my mind of birds and other animals and trees dying that way. My thinly considered notion had been that hunters, men and other animals, were the killing agents for all God's creatures great and small.

Now that some other understanding of its fate had come into my mind, a measure of all-too-human romantic fantasy swirled into the mix and I looked again at the tern's dark eyes and thought I saw sadness.

I set down my bucket and knelt on the sand, my hands on my knees. I looked at the tern, and it continued to eye me. Then it, too, went down, but more heavily than I, its round breast cradled by the sand. I studied the bird, and I couldn't sustain the belief that I beheld sadness there. It was merely my own sentimentality at play. Then I remembered what Walt Whitman had said in a poem that always sounded to me like a prayer:

"... O to be self-balanced for contingencies,

"To confront night, storms, hunger, ridicule, accidents and rebuffs as the trees and animals do."

And this tern was, in fact, being rebuffed, ignored by another tern like it not twenty yards away. It had found a scrap of bread on the beach and was pecking away at it, oblivious of his kin's pain. None of this "There, but for the grace of God, go I" stuff.

Shakespeare had Hamlet say that a thing is neither good nor bad, that only thinking makes it so. I tried to put aside my thinking, my eye for romance. The tern was sick or dying, and that was neither good nor bad. It just was.

To confront, then, this night alone, not crying out for alms or solace at the approach of descending darkness, thin December air whipping through gray-boned trees, to face death quietly under silent stars, that is what men have sought and where saints rejoice.

When Descartes said he thought therefore he was, he did not add that because he thought, therefore he was in danger of the hellfire of thinking. When the tern blinked and turned its head, I stood and picked up my net bucket. There was nothing for me to do except pry myself out of my maudlin reverie. Nothing to do but walk to my boat, whose name, it occurred to me, was the *Sea Bird.* A sailor more superstitious than I might count the dying tern an omen of a course wrongly set, a metaphor set before me to point me home. But I was not a believer in intercessory magic.

I turned to go and was startled to come face-to-face

with a gaunt man in a floppy hat carrying a broad black leather portfolio under his arm, fat with loose drawing papers. If I was such a certain unbeliever, why had a shiver run down my spine? I drew in a breath and squared my shoulders, and almost as quickly found a trace of humor in the picture of myself so taken aback by this sojourner on the twilight beach. A pigment-splattered wooden box with a handle like a suitcase for his pens and paints and brushes hung at his side in the curl of his right hand.

He was taller than I, shabbily dressed, and, superstition or no, I would have thought him a forbidding character, except that I could see his eyes, and they were alight with unmistakable goodwill. I saw something else there in his eyes that was volatile and capricious, but more a shadow than a light, now dormant, but as full of possibility as an egg in a nest.

"You would like to help the bird," he said.

"I don't know what I'd do," I said.

"I didn't ask you what you'd do. I merely observed that I believe you want to do something."

"Yes, sir. I thought about it."

"And that is enough, you know. If it were a man, you should perhaps explore further what may be done. But with this tern, who does not want or need your help, it is enough that you wished to offer assistance."

"But what good comes of doing absolutely nothing?" I was becoming vexed with the stranger's condescending attitude. What could he really know of what the mute bird on the beach desired of me? It angered me that he presumed to teach me something that he could not possibly know.

"Oh, you haven't done *nothing*," the painter said, wagging one of the fingers that was holding his paint box. "Do you remember your Bible lesson that having done something in the mind, having fantasized about stealing your friend's girlfriend was a sin on the order of having actually taken the lass for a stroll on this beach and kissing her?"

"I remember talk like that when the sermon was about coveting."

"Well, talk in church is often about the wrong that you do. For you know," and he grinned broadly, "it is the evil men do that lives after them, and what pitiful good they deign to cobble together is oft interred with their bones."

"I thought you were talking about the Bible," I said. "Now you've switched to Shakespeare."

"Well, they both speak Elizabethan English, right?"

"Unless we use the Greek, or Aramaic texts."

"Touché," the painter said with a slight bow of his head. "You've wounded me, young sir. But not to the death, so I shall finish my point: If it is true that you should not covet, because it is a sin to commit a wrongful deed even in thought, then it is also a virtue to commit a rightful deed even in thought."

He paused, still gazing at me.

"Do you agree with that?"

"It seems consistent."

"Well said. Excellent!" He grinned broadly. "That is why I don't go to church. I think about it, and that's enough!" He laughed a great loud laugh, and I instinctively looked to see if the tern had been startled by this strange honking call of the intruding two-legged beast. It did not move. I looked back at the painter. He was waiting for me to speak. Something, the light in his eyes, his edgy intelligence, that big laugh, something about this man caused me to like him. But I didn't know what to say, settling for an easy query about him couched as an observation.

"I haven't seen you around Fairhope before."

"No. My brother Peter is a potter and loves to come here to get clay down by your Fish River. To him it's like a vein of gold there. We live on the coast of Mississippi, at Ocean Springs. I decided to come to Fairhope and see what all his fuss was about it."

"Well, all the fuss now in Fairhope is the same fuss as all over the country."

"The war?"

"Yes," I said.

"And that is another thing about which I know not what to do."

"I should introduce you to my father. His idea is to attack the only German citizen of Fairhope. My mother's idea is to harbor him."

I couldn't believe I'd just said that to a stranger. I was nonplussed about how to back out of that one. But the artist let it slip mercifully past.

"German and Japanese Americans will suffer. It is not fair. But you cannot help them, I'm afraid."

"Like I can't help the bird?" I asked. Like I can't help myself, I thought.

"Not at all like that. If we humans were a hive, or a herd, or a flock, truly, you would have some fair hope of success. But we are self-righteously individualistic and are wont to love our own fears first."

He nodded up the beach.

"My boat's just up there a ways," he said. "Will you walk with me? This tern needs his privacy. He has some dying to do."

"My boat's in the creek. I'm going that way," I said. Some dying to do? And why not? The painter's remark wrapped itself tightly around my brain. I could tell the painter was giving the topic of the war a rest when he made a subtle shift and asked about my cast net.

"You don't have any fish there in your bucket?"

"No. I didn't even make a cast." I kicked sand ahead of me. "I just walked today." Walked and dragged along with me ever more complete images of my mother's involvement with Josef Unruh. Frazzle-headed over what it meant that Anna Pearl caught them holding hands.

I'd seen my mother and my father, too, embrace other men, other women. I'd seen my mother tilt her face to receive a kiss on the cheek. I'd seen my father bestow that same kiss on the cheek of women I did not know. But all these displays of affection had been in public, usually at church, sometimes at chance meetings outside a storefront in Fairhope. It was the privacy of Mother's deed that seemed to corroborate all of Anna Pearl's insinuations, and all but completely erode my own hopeful denial.

"My name is Walter Anderson." He stopped and set down his box of paints and extended his hand.

"Rove MacNee."

"You live here, Rove?"

"Yes, south of here. My family has a house. I, uh, well—"

For some reason, it seemed suddenly an odd thing to say that I had moved out of a house and onto a sailboat.

"You don't live with your family in that house?"

"Not at the moment," I said, fumbling. "The boat I mentioned, well, I moved aboard it a few days ago."

"Well, then, I am pleased to meet a brother boat-dweller," the painter said. "I have a house, too, in Ocean Springs. But I live now at a place with the rather bucolic-sounding name of Oldfields near Gautier. In fact, I have a family in that house." Walter Anderson paused, as if going to his family in his mind. "But I have discovered," he continued, "that I enjoy living underneath my boat. And I'm taking that joy on farther and wider expeditions. My bounty is growing. This landfall has been a good one."

"Even with all the nervous uncertainty about the war?" I asked.

"Oh, the fuss here is about far more than the war. You have some real fringe-dwellers living in this town. Do you know how rare are these fringe-dwellers?"

I'd heard that kind of talk before, at school, on the

porches, about the eccentric types attracted to Fairhope. And here was another.

"And do you count yourself one of them, living underneath your boat?" I asked.

"Of course I do. Here, I'll show you my fringe dwelling," he offered. "It's just up the beach here."

As we walked, Walter Anderson talked about netfishing. "From the first moment in my own boyhood when I watched a bent old man swirl a perfect circle of net out over the water, I've been in awe of those who throw the net well. To me it is art in motion. The most grizzled old coot working his net is easily as graceful as a ballet dancer, and I have thought many times to carve a net fisherman. He'd have to be poised for the throw, you see." Walter Anderson seemed to consider this. "Unless I did a mixed-media representation," he paused, "and made the hoop of net from silver filament." He stopped walking and I could tell he was making a mental note. He seemed in a trance.

When he began walking across the sand again, the artist told me that when a mullet net is gathered right, when the toss is executed precisely, it is a poem of form and movement. "And catching a mullet for the frying pan is merely God's extra measure," the artist said.

I remember clearly an evening when I had gone down on the Big Pier with Father Brown and we stopped at a spot along the rail deemed the right spot by the priest.

"Watch me closely," he had said. "I'm not going to be telling you anything. Just watch me." This was the first time that the priest and I had gone alone with our nets to the dock, the first time he had offered me instruction. I watched him take his net from the bucket he carried. I left mine in the bucket at my feet.

First, he secured the net's leader rope to his left wrist by cinching a small loop. Then the priest coiled the rest of the leader into his left hand. Lifting his net from the pier, it dangled from eye level to his bare toes.

The first three feet of the bunched net, he pulled into a gentle loop that joined the coils of leader in his left hand. The tail end of the rest of the net hung down three feet, which he called the skirt. He looked at me, as if to ask if I saw the sense of this scheme of rope and net, looped and spread and divided. I did. And I have never forgotten.

Then he took the hem of the skirt into his mouth, with two of the many evenly spaced lead weights hanging just out of his mouth, and gently, by using the back of his right hand in a fanning motion, he divided the skirt into equal parts by flipping some of it over his right forearm. Now he held his net one part in his left hand and one part in his right hand, the middle of the hem still hanging from his mouth.

"Now," Father Brown muttered around the net in his mouth as he walked up to the rail and looked over at the water. The bay was slick. Twilight softened everything, and helped paint the scene onto my memory.

"There," he said, nodding toward the water beneath him. He looked to me like an old osprey eyeing its prey. He tensed his muscles and stepped back from the rail a half step. He planted his feet and twisted his torso slightly, cocking his body for the toss, and without pause ghosted back up to the rail with a slow rotation that sent the net flying, just clearing the rail at his waist. It swooshed into the growing dusk and fell toward the water, a sixteen-foot perfect circle of net tied to a man's wrist. "They're in there," he said. And they were. And so was I, caught and christened by the good father, converted to a calling, baptized in the sea-smelling water that drips from a mullet net.

I was surprised that I hadn't seen the painter's boat when I'd come by earlier, but, almost as if reading my thoughts, he said, "I sailed in here while you were walking down the beach. I saw you as I came in. I did three watercolors and several drawings of the royal tern while you were walkabout."

My father had told me the Aborigine term for walking the outback on a vision quest, and I wondered if the artist could discern that my compass, just now, pointed adrift. It was interesting to me how fluid was the swing from enthusiasm to feeling a lack of purpose, how erratic my philosophical bearings in this short turn out of my father and mother's house. I walked behind the artist and noticed how his head would turn this way and that, how his pace would slow if he looked off in the same direction for long, and I believed he was framing the visible world with a poet's imagination.

It would soon be dark, and I was glad for enough light to see Walter Anderson's boat. It was basically a hard-

chined sailing dinghy that at other times was a rowing
skiff. The oarlocks were fixed into the gunwales, and the
oars were leaned against the hull. I guessed the boat was
about sixteen feet long, maybe six feet wide. It was fitted
with oarlocks and a mast with a loose-footed sail. He had
it dragged ten yards up on the beach. We walked up beside
the boat, and he set down his painter's things. He un-
stepped the mast and flipped over his boat. He propped up
its one side with the tiller handle, which he had slipped
from its fitting atop the rudder.

"Thirty minutes of scooping out and banking sand
and underneath this very boat is a lovely shelter. Quite
cozy. With a blanket on the sand, what more could a man
ask for?" He lifted his hand, pointing his finger upward.
"Well, in truth, if the damnable gnats and mosquitoes
come, I do have need for more."

The artist told me he'd stopped off at some islands on
the way here, two nights on Horn Island, another on Petit
Bois, two nights on Dauphin Island. "On Petit Bois," he
said, scratching his neck as if to illustrate the point, "I was
bitten so severely by gnats that my head swelled to near
twice its size."

He put down his things, opened his portfolio, and took
out three random drawings. He studied them for a moment, then handed them to me. Even in the dimness I
could detect in these pen-and-ink line drawings an exquisite eye and an obedient hand in this artist.

I set down my bucket and took the drawings into both
hands and brought the pages near my face. I became so

lost in the work, so drawn into the alchemy of creation that I was transfixed, almost hypnotized. I could not fathom how a simple line on a white piece of paper could be so alive and read so magically of movement and life and mystery. I was completely arrested.

"These are beautiful," was all I could think to say, and in a weak voice.

But Walter Anderson was not there. He had walked away. I blinked and turned my face from the drawings to look around. There he was down the beach in the direction from which we had just come. He was kneeling on the sand within arm's length of the tern, his hat in his hand. In the magic-colored light of approaching dusk, the sun just gone below the tree line across the bay at Dog River, here was this strange rumpled man down like a magi in prayer scooping up a wounded bird in his hat.

It was time for me to go and leave Walter Anderson. He had already left me and was in that different room of the world where he lived, where his eye saw and his hand rendered so perfectly what the light caressed and brought to life in colors and shapes.

I put my hand against the trunk of a stout cypress and raised myself to standing while holding in my other hand the drawings, careful with them. All that was left of the sun was awash on the western rim of the sky and quickly fading. The breeze was freshening and the temperature was sliding down. I said nothing to the artist, but only walked away, stopping twice to look back at him still on his knees, his catch held to his breast.

Back at home aboard the *Sea Bird,* I opened the small portlight above the counter in the main cabin. I lit a gimbaled kerosene lamp. Night bugs were making a racket, and a skinny-legged, dappled spider crawled down the lamp and dropped on a thin filament to the counter. He went right to work making a small web, daring me to fool with him.

I listened into the night as it settled over my place on Fly Creek. Water was dripping somewhere. A mullet belly-flopped near the stern. The night and all in it, mindless of contingencies.

But, not me. I reached for my logbook and pencil on the shelf, and wrote: "I know about things like night and storms and hunger. I want to bend things my way, fend off God and control the contingencies, to meet them and master them. I wonder if sixty years more will be enough to unlearn my fears so far. I wonder if I'll someday want to set things on a proper axis for others, but give up such a tilting at windmills."

I leaned back on the starboard settee and propped my feet on the port side berth, watching the spider work. I put down my logbook and put my hands behind my head and closed my eyes and let the night noises on Fly Creek surround me, close down my thinking. If I was waiting for an epiphany from my run-in with the artist down on the beach, it never came. And I could be sure that the sadness I felt was my own.

Carlton Smith had told Anna Pearl and me that the crack in the *Sea Bird*'s boom was more cosmetic than structural. His prognosis was years of good service, so she and I had brought the boom back to the boat and laid it on the deck.

Then after coffee and dry toast with some honey in the cockpit, Anna Pearl left, and I returned to work, spending the morning refitting my boom. I shackled it to the gooseneck on the mast, then hanked on the mainsail. I then adjusted the tension on the shrouds and stays to balance the mast side to side, and fore and aft, with a little aft rake for better windward performance. My father had taught me how to tune a boat's rigging with the same patient voice and unhurried manner he used in our best days together in the woodshop.

"When your mast is standing fair port to starboard, then loosen the forestay and tighten the backstay until you've got her raked three to five degrees," the captain had told me.

"This will give you more bite at the helm," he

said. "She'll be wanting to swing harder and faster to weather, which will bring your bow on the wind and luff your sails." He told me that a boat not properly tuned for a weather helm means your boat will keep sailing away from you should you fall overboard. "Sloppy tuning is reckless and dangerous," the captain warned.

I was a quick study on the *Mary Foster*. I saw the sense of each task within moments of its due deliberation. As a boy on deck, I'd watched a sailor handling and making up lines so quickly that it looked almost showy, or even comical. Then my father had caught me observing the same man monkeyed out on the bowsprit coiling the anchor rode and guiding it through a chock. The limber man moved like the boat behind him was on fire. But the winds were light and the boat was sailing steadily.

"What's his rush, Rove?" the captain queried, his hands controlling the helm, his eye fixed out past the bow.

"So when there's a real need, it's second nature to him."

"And when will there be a real need, as you say, Son?"

"No one can say, sir."

"Only God in his heaven, boy! And he'll not wait for you to shake the sleep from your eyes."

So I had carefully accomplished the tuning and adjustment of my sloop's standing rigging to correct tolerances. I'd suited her up in sails, hoisted and lowered them, stowed the jib in a yankee bag on the foredeck, and secured the main with a canvas boom cover.

I sat down in the cockpit and leaned back against the coaming. I was watching a loon diving and playing in the middle of the creek when my eyelids grew heavy, and I felt a buzz in my head. I'd not eaten since breakfast and was hungry, but decided to go below and take a nap.

I had tossed out the dank cotton mattress my first day on the *Sea Bird* and folded two blankets into a pad to soften the wooden shelf on which I would lie up toward the bow of my boat. Before I lay down, I opened the overhead hatch, letting light and fresh air into the forward salon. Almost by the time I was prone, I was asleep, my cheek caressed by the indigo woolen blanket I'd slept on as long as I could remember. My father had brought me the plain, soft blanket from a French Market stall in the Quarter close to the levee.

When my father's voice tumbled into the open hatch, it might have been a dream caught on the moment, invading my nap. When it came the second time, with more volume and belligerence, I got up quickly, still woozy.

"Sir?" I called up through the open hatch, moving aft in the cabin, making for the open companionway. I popped my head up from the cabin and saw my father standing, arms crossed, near where the painter was wrapped around the sycamore. He was dressed in a fine woolen coat, buttoned to the neck, his beard trimmed and his boots shining. I did not see the Buick.

"Did Father Brown come here yesterday?" the captain asked, his eyes smoldering black. "Did he tell you that I said for you to come home before sunset?"

Of course my father knew the answer, and there was only one reply for me to give.

"Yes, sir."

"And you chose to ignore my request?"

"No, sir." I spoke evenly, my voice strong, actually looking at my father as an adversary, and weighing the possible
outcome of a physical fight with him. "I did not ignore
your request, Father. I decided that I'm at home on my
boat. I decided not to leave it."

"And if I come aboard your vessel and drag you ashore
and down the beach to *my* house?"

"I don't want you to do that, Father."

"Why should I not?" The captain uncrossed his arms
and placed his hands on his hips, his feet wide apart.

I stood on the cockpit seat, putting my right hand on
the boom cover. "I'd fight you if you tried." I felt the con-
striction of my throat and willed back the tears.

"You may be right, Son. You're a man now." My father stood unmoving like the massive hundred-foot-tall
slash pine close beside him on his right. "You've collected
your birthright strength and stubbornness from me. But
you cannot best me in a fight. Don't think you can. You
watched the German make that mistake."

The captain dropped his hands, hooking the thumb of
his right hand into the waistband of his breeches. He took
two steps nearer the boat. "If you fought me like a man,
Rove, I would batter you without hesitation."

I blinked. Dominus MacNee meant every word he
said, and something about speaking those words to me
seemed to effect a kind of catharsis for him. He looked to

his right, then up the pine. He dropped his eyes to a spot up the creek and reached inside his big coat for his pipe and some tobacco. When he'd loaded, tamped, and lit the pipe, he said, "Father Brown said you talk of joining the navy."

This surprised me. I'd told only Anna Pearl. Had she told her mother, and Miss Anderson told Father Brown? Or had Anna Pearl told him herself? I hoped it had been talk between a mother and daughter that ultimately brought this information to my father. I didn't want to think that Anna Pearl was such an easy talker with things I said. On the other hand, I hadn't asked her to keep in confidence this notion about enlisting.

"I've thought about it, yes, sir."

"I was fifteen at the end of the last war with Germany." My father's face relaxed; he seemed to be drifting in contemplation. "It would have been an honor to draw a sword against the Kaiser's army."

I did not feel a call to honor; I felt a sense of duty on behalf of innocence, its ceremonies threatened by Yeats's "blood-dimmed tide." "I would fight to stop Hitler. He *is* that 'rough beast slouching toward Bethlehem,' Father."

"That's a right reading of 'The Second Coming,' Son." I remembered the position held by my father in the argument with Josef Unruh, but his comment was neither conciliatory nor gratuitous. "I must say I'm surprised, Rove." The captain halted and looked up toward the sky. He put his pipe in his teeth, clasped his hands behind his back, and stared at me for a moment. "No. It doesn't surprise me, Son," he said, speaking around his pipe. "I'm proud of you."

I steadied my breathing, but my heart would not answer my call to be still. My father had not regarded me in this manner, had not spoken to me in this tone in three years. I could say nothing. I blinked and gripped the canvas of the boom cover tightly.

My father took his pipe from his mouth and said, "My ship has a short list of repairs that are in order. It's been almost a year since I put her in the yards, and merchant vessels might be called upon to aid the war effort. The *Mary Foster* will be ready. I need you on deck with me to sail her to Bayou La Batre. I told my men they were off for Christmas. I've hired Blue for this trip, but I need another hand. Will you sail with me?"

Under the circumstances, there was only one answer. "I will," I said.

"Excellent," said the captain, and he made as if to turn and go, but then he stopped and began looking at the *Sea Bird.* I watched his eyes light up as they swept the sheer of the deck, appraised the fine entry of the bow, let his gaze drift upward to the spars and rigging. "Have you sailed her?"

"No, sir."

"Well, she's not a fishing skiff. Get her out of this creek." The captain walked step by slow step toward the stern of the *Sea Bird,* continuing his survey of her scantlings, lines, and rigging, gauging her seaworthiness. "Bring your boat off the pier at Magnolia Bayhouse. She draws what, three and a half feet?"

"Three foot nine."

"Bring her in a little south of the crabbing pier, thirty yards out. Drop the hook and pay out sixty feet of rode." The captain looked me in the eye, and I stood up straight, a sailor before the officer on deck.

"I'd like to sail to Bosarge's yard in Bayou La Batre day after tomorrow," he said. "You will earn a full wage." My father and I held each other in a locked gaze.

"I'll sail in before sunset tomorrow," I said. I didn't say that I'd promised Anna Pearl an invitation for the maiden voyage of *Sea Bird*. I was not at all certain that she'd come along. On the other hand, the possibility made me hopeful.

"Your mother will have supper on the table when you come ashore." The captain nodded, a finger to his brow in casual salute, and walked away up the hill, angling toward the south along the higher ridge of the creek bank underneath the taller, older thick-butted trees unfazed by the sometime-floods on Fly Creek. The captain's course suggested to me that he might have walked all the way here, and the tightening that wouldn't go away in my chest and throat suggested I was not yet the stoical young man I thought I was.

Sea Bird *made* good headway, and gracefully, moving so easily it was as though she wanted to get out of the creek and into open water where she belonged. The little waves that fell off the sides of her bow sinuously punctuated our going and raised an excited whisper to the green of the trees and the land she was leaving behind. I worked the long sculling oar over the stern, my left hand on the tiller.

Anna Pearl had come by yesterday as she'd promised and jumped at the chance to sail with me. She'd donned woolen trousers and waistcoat for the wintry sail down the bay to Magnolia Bayhouse pier. Her clothes were baggy, but I noted with appreciation her curves when she bent to pull the oar through the water from her stance on the bow. I would never be so bold, except that she was turned away from me.

"Keep your eye on the creek, Captain," she said, knowing in that strange way a woman knows when she is being observed.

God! That girl. How could I have known then that she was not a ship of Longfellow's passing me in the night, that her face would now and again appear and fill my mind and spin me back down the decades, or sometimes my recall was hazy, more like trying to remember the scent of a rose.

When the *Sea Bird*'s bowsprit pointed around the last bend in Fly Creek before the fishing docks, I felt enough wind on my neck, fluky though it was, that I believed we could sail out the mouth of the creek. The wind was out of the north at less than ten knots. Nice and easy for my first sail, and that suited me just fine. My heart was hammering hard enough just to be under way in my boat.

I told Anna Pearl that we'd clear the shrimping boats so I could bring the bow around on the wind and hoist the mainsail, keeping the boom amidships and the wind out of the sails for a moment. I wouldn't have to leave the tiller, and Anna Pearl could stay put on the foredeck in this light air.

"What do I need to do?" she asked me as we slipped past a fifty-foot Biloxi lugger laid alongside the dock. Things were quiet on the waterfront this time of year with Christmas so close. I was pleased there weren't many people around to see my first sail-handling and maneuvers aboard *Sea Bird.* The boat was ready, but I wasn't sure I was. My stomach was shaky. Anna Pearl, on the other hand, would not have been more at ease if she had been sitting in her front porch swing.

"I'll head over there where there's plenty of room and jibe her, bring her around, and head into the wind," I said by way of preparing her. "You don't need to do anything."

"You want me to handle the jib? That way we can get both sails up at the same time," Anna Pearl said.

"That would be a good idea," I said, pleased, but not surprised, that she would know the right sail-handling tactic. "We might have to backwind the jib to fall off and get some headway. Let's do it. I'm coming about."

She jumped back in the cockpit, slipping her oar through the open hatch into the cabin, and reached for a coil of line. I was about to tell her that the jib and halyard were words for foresail and the line that hauled it up, but she looked up to the top of the mast, let her eye follow the lines downward, and grabbed the correct coil, uncleated it, and dropped the end of the line in the cockpit beside her.

"Got it," she said. "Ready on the jib, Skipper."

I took one more good pull on my sculling oar and handed it to Anna Pearl. She put it away with the other one. I'd secure them both later when we were sailing. The fetch from my heavy stroke carried the bow right around, and I let go the tiller and with both hands quickly grabbed the mainsail halyard. Anna Pearl let me get the main a third of the way up the mast before she began hauling up on the jib, then, in unison and in less than ten seconds both sails were up and cleated. I got back to the tiller while Anna Pearl made up the tails of the halyards. I eased the tiller to starboard and the bow fell away to port. I cleated off the main, and the sail ballooned and filled with air. The *Sea Bird* lurched ahead. Anna Pearl was about to cleat the jib sheet, and I told her to hold off.

"Just half a minute," I said. "Let me get some headway so we've got steerage. If you cleat it now, it'll pull our bow off the wind too hard. Ease it in. Easy. A little more." The sloop heeled to port and gave another jump forward. "Now! Haul it in and cleat it off."

I moved to port in the cockpit to increase our angle of heel just a little, increasing our efficiency through the water. Anna Pearl was still standing, her hands on the cabin roof, adjusting her position to help our balance and speed. I eased the main, and it took a better shape and we got another knot of speed.

My heart was pounding. The *Sea Bird* was behaving like a living thing bounding for open water. We got a gust and I shifted my weight quickly to starboard, grinning like a five-year-old on Christmas morning. All the work and anticipation and delay came down to just this. All the sorry drama at Magnolia Bayhouse in this moment, *for* this moment, vanished behind the curtain of this magic show.

There is nothing that can equal the response of the mind and muscles to a sleek boat swept along before the wind, responding to the lift and drag and thrust of the breeze as a bird on the wing. No coughing, growling motor exhausting its blue and stifling smoke.

This was silent movement as clean as falling snowflakes. This was motion that felt each nuance of the wind driving it, a dance of exquisite rapport between man and nature. The bow rising over a wave, the stern settling into the trough, wind and spray in your hair and lungs, and a hobbyhorse switch-up: Now a settling of the bow into green water and the rising up and up of the stern, up and over the crest of a sliding wave, and the swish and splash of the bubbling wake as the *Sea Bird* sped forward.

Anna Pearl looked back at me. "We did that well."

"Yes, we did," I said, feathering the tiller to keep the sloop in the middle of the creek as we covered the last fifty yards before breaking out into the bay. "With skill and grace, I'd venture to say."

"As though it was practiced," she said, turning and taking a seat on the high side toward the front of the cockpit and leaning her back against the coaming. She put her feet up on the seat across from her. She had on pleated-front black wool pants and a baggy cable-knit sweater. Her low-top lace-up boots looked like a boy's. She looked altogether satisfied to be just where she was.

"Thank you, Rove, for inviting me along. I'm honored," she said.

"Let's see if you still say that when you get off the boat," I said.

Sea Bird dipped her lee rail in a gust and bounded ahead, past the breakwater at the mouth of the creek and into the open bay. Without the least hesitation I let fly a wild yell as the sloop chased off to the west on a broad reach.

Aye yeeee!

We were heeling seven degrees to port, the sails full and pulling like a team of horses. The wind was steady at ten knots, with some gusts. At that moment, anointed by hormones from my adrenal medulla, I could have, would have, sailed like Joshua Slocum all the way to the edge of the world, taking my lovely hostage on a voyage chasing after the setting sun.

I was so lost in the joy of this first sail aboard my boat, after almost two years' wait and countless hours of work, that I did not see the artist's work-skiff coming abreast of me. His call, a bellow, really, over the wind and waves, startled me, and I inadvertently pushed the tiller away from me to break our headway, as if a collision were imminent. Not that a wreck would damage Walter Anderson's sad-looking boat, with its ragged and dingy sail loose-footed on a slightly bent, willowy boom.

"Rove?" Anna Pearl, herself taken by surprise, spoke my name as if calling for an explanation about what was going on here. There was no time to go into my brief meeting with this pirate-looking fellow bearing down on us. I'd fill her in later.

"The tern died! I buried him," Walter Anderson called out to me. He drew nearer, a reckless maneuver since I'd luffed my sails in my own bad move at the tiller. My sloop seemed about to go into irons. I didn't have good control of my boat and could not avoid crashing into him if he got closer. I motioned for him to stand off, and he expertly jibed his boat, hauling in on the main sheet to manage the boom, then easing it out as it crossed his head. His tactic let me get ahead of him several boat lengths, so he yelled again. "Heave to! Can you heave her to?"

My father had taught me how to bring a boat hove-to. It was like an act of sorcery to me, as a young boy, to manipulate the tiller and headsails on a sailboat in such a way that, with all the sails flying, even in a hard blow, you could bring the boat to a virtual standstill.

It immediately occurred to me that, like Tom walking the fence for Becky Thatcher, this might really impress Anna Pearl. She was attentive and a quick study, and I knew she'd find it intriguing.

"What's he talking about, Rove?"

"I'll show you." I pushed the tiller over and fell off the wind enough to regain headway. When she was moving well, I said, "Ready about!"

That was the call for her to get ready on the jib sheet and to be mindful of the boom and the change in balance to a starboard angle of heel. Anna Pearl prepared to let go the sheet on the port side and made ready to haul in on the starboard jib sheet.

"No, we won't bring the jib across. When I bring the bow across the wind, I want you to harden up on that sheet."

"And backwind the jib?"

"And backwind the jib," I said.

"But—"

"You'll see," I said.

"Ready about." I repeated the command. "Coming about," I said, pushing the tiller smoothly over, and the *Sea Bird*'s bowsprit turned toward the western horizon. When we'd crossed the apparent wind, I let the sloop come on around another ten degrees until the wind began to catch and fill the backside of the jib.

"Now! Haul in hard!"

She did so, and the wind gave the boat a spin. But I met the spinning effort of the wind on the bow with an opposite force on the rudder by shoving it hard to leeward. The wind wanted to push *Sea Bird* one way, the rudder wanted to steer her in the opposite direction. The effect was to stall the boat. The only motion was a little sideways slide, leeway with a slight heel. The boat bobbed in the water, almost still and comfortably stable on deck.

"Amazing!" Anna Pearl said,

"At your service, ma'am," I answered, completely pleased.

"Nice job," came the voice of the artist, now almost alongside. He let go his main and jib sheet and let his sails luff. He swept his rudder back and forth with great energy a couple of times and stalled his own boat by putting it in irons. And since the wind was not strong, it was entirely manageable for him. Especially since he'd come up on the lee side of us in our windshadow.

"Did you hear me say the tern died?" The painter moved to the bow of his boat and took hold of the gunwale of the *Sea Bird*. His hands were rough and calloused, belying the gentle art they made.

"Hello," he said, before I could answer, nodding to Anna Pearl. "My name is Walter Anderson. I am a friend of your captain."

I liked the sound of "your captain" in relation to my passenger. She looked at me with her eyebrows arched.

"Mr. Anderson is an artist," I told her, "a painter from Ocean Springs, Mississippi. He sailed here in his fine boat." Anna Pearl's face said she would hardly risk sailing across the bay in the artist's boat. He smiled at her.

"I'd sail this dinghy to Cozumel without a second thought," he said. And, without reserve, I believed him. Here was the real brother of Huck Finn and Joshua Slocum and ragtag sailors who own the moving waters of the world.

I said to Mr. Anderson, "I heard you say the tern died and that you buried him."

"On the beach. I marked its grave with a cross of driftwood. I administered proper burial rites." The painter was not at all insincere. His face turned to follow the low flight of a pelican, so focused that he might have been in that moment spirited off his boat and was now following the broad-winged fisherman over the waves.

Anna Pearl waited until he returned his attention in our direction, then, and with serious intent, asked, "What bird was it that died?"

"I met Mr. MacNee here as we both studied an old royal tern on the beach over there."

He gestured across the water toward the strip of sand and junipers a mile to the east of us. The painter's dinghy held to the side of the *Sea Bird* even though the artist had let go his handhold. It seemed caught in an eddy downwind of my boat, and the two boats drifted in an easy leeway.

"I had already done several drawings of the old man, the bird, and was about to offer my hand to it, when I saw your captain walking my way. I waited and watched him, and then found myself studying the captain studying the bird. I decided then that I like this Rove MacNee." Walter Anderson looked at me, then back to Anna Pearl. "And I've spoiled your sail just to tell him the rest of the bird's story."

"Nothing is spoiled, Mr. Anderson. Thank you for letting me know," I said.

"You are welcome," he said, massaging the stubble on his chin. "But, mostly, I wanted to tell you that I am sailing out of Mobile Bay tomorrow morning. I came to see what Peter was raving about in your Fairhope. And, I have seen much of what captures his affection."

Walter Anderson clapped his hands once, loudly, a gesture of excitement.

"And this morning I was treated to an astounding gift, a miracle that I had heard of and, quite frankly, found all but impossible to believe when my brother spoke of it."

I knew what he was going to say, so I asked him, "Was there a jubilee this morning?"

"A spectacular display of God's bounty and incredible sense of humor," he said. Walter Anderson had seen his first jubilee, an odd phenomenon where crabs and flounder and shrimp and eels, all the bottom dwellers, by the hundreds or thousands, swim into the shallow water at the shore and languish there while citizens respond by coming to the beach with buckets and tubs and taking home fresh seafood in shameful quantities.

No one knows when a jubilee will happen, day or night, and it usually doesn't last for long. We were taught at the Organic School that jubilees occur at only two places on earth: on the Spanish shores of the Mediterranean and on the Eastern Shore of Mobile Bay.

"I said I came to see what all the buzz is about, and I find someone hereabouts is buzzing the fish with electricity," he said with a wry smile, watching Anna Pearl. She looked confused.

"There are people," I told her, "who fish for catfish on the inland rivers by 'telephoning' for them. They take a telephone's wind-up electrical device and attach wires to it and drop them down to the bottom of the river. When they turn the crank, the jolt of electricity stuns the catfish and they float to the surface for easy gathering."

"That doesn't sound like fair play," Anna Pearl said with some agitation.

"Oh, it is absolutely illegal poaching," Walter Anderson said.

"It should be," Anna Pearl replied.

"But I know this jubilee is surely the work of the Fisherman himself. I thanked Him when I took one flounder for my breakfast fire. It was the fattest, juiciest, whitest, and sweetest fish meat I have ever eaten." Walter Anderson grew silent again and looked across the broad water toward Dog River on the western shore of the bay.

"Do you have enough provisions to get you home?" There was nothing at all in his boat at that moment, save his canvas bag with his paper and drawing things inside. "I guess you're sailing to Oldfields?"

"I will get there eventually," he replied. "I'll stop at Horn Island for a spell. And, yes, I have plenty to eat. A bowl of rice and a can of sardines is never in short supply aboard my courageous vessel."

Walter Anderson patted roughly the broad board seat upon which he sat, and drifted again into a contemplative silence.

"Do you know, many fat, well-fed citizens of the Gulf Coast here would be surprised what jubilee awaits them almost every day down at the seashore. Not your piles of fish and crabs, sir, but the bounty that washes ashore. I have retrieved whole stalks of bananas, doubtless lost over the side of a banana boat sailing from New Orleans to Mobile." The painter got a merry twinkle in his eye. "Canned goods with labels washed away make for a meal and a surprise all in one."

Anna Pearl was delighted with the man in the dinghy and could not keep back a wistful tone. "What an adventure! Grocery shopping in the island surf."

"And no shifty-eyed merchant totting up his list," said Walter Anderson.

"You are a lucky man, Mr. Anderson," I said, "to be provisioned on your excursions without having to load down your boat with supplies."

He leaned to the side, tipping his boat, swirling his hand in the water, watching intently the effect, it seemed, of the play of the light on the ripples he stirred. Then, without raising his head, he turned his face to look at me in much the way a bird cocks its head and one-eyes the object of its wonder.

"I am a child of fortune, my boy," he said. "Favored by Providence merely because I expect it. Do you understand? Thoreau wrote that our focus determines our reality. Knock and the door shall be opened, Captain MacNee."

Hearing the title and name of my father proffered in my own direction had an immediate effect upon me of a kind of dread, felt as an electrical tingling in the lower part of my stomach. But it was not born of my usual contempt for his whiskey-logged and reddened face being too close to mine. Captain Dominus MacNee, if he admitted to himself what he would allow himself only to suspect— his wife's familiarity with Josef Unruh—he would kill him. My mother's fate would depend on her proximity to the captain's act of revenge: At arm's length, she, too, would suffer. I lost the moment.

Anna Pearl and *Sea Bird* and Walter Anderson and their arrangement together were with me on this dreamy canvas of sunshot hues, all rendered in pigment so pure and perfect that the crimson could have been stolen from a heart chamber, the cerulean called down from the cloudless sky, and all in a blink it was smeared and run together, and the whole mess dropped overboard.

"I expect we'd better sail on, Mr. Anderson," I said, a set coming into my jaw as my eyes reached down the bay toward the pier at Magnolia Bayhouse. "My father is expecting me."

Both Anna Pearl and the painter picked up on the swift transformation in my demeanor and, though neither could possibly have guessed at what had darkly moved me, both allowed it. Anna Pearl said nothing as she straightened her back and looked idly up at the full sails. When she let her eyes come to mine, I knew she had looked cautiously into the chasm wherein I'd just fallen.

Curiously, the artist slung water droplets on me and said, "Child of fortune, I am. Fortune's favorite son, Rove MacNee. When the gods and demons get to wrestling so in your back pocket, boy, sail away. The wind is free, the water is wide. I'll be camped on Horn Island. If you come there, I will draw your boat."

It sounded so absurd, that I would implement such a journey on *Sea Bird* for the sake of a drawing, and yet two words sprang immediately to my mind with the force of a biblical exhortation to *go forth:* "Why not?"

I had no good answer for the question, so I said nothing.

The wind had come up as we'd closed the distance on the pier at Magnolia Bayhouse and quickly built a chop that ran almost three feet, with whitecaps being blown off. Anna Pearl and I had both got wet. My father met us on the end of the dock and watched while I made the tricky maneuver to come alongside the boards so Anna Pearl could get off the boat. The sails were down and I had to scull the boat with a long oar.

"I watched you handling the sloop coming in. She was easy under your hand. When you jibed her and put her bow into the wind, you got the sails down as fast as any of my crew on the *Mary Foster*," the captain said.

"And Anna Pearl—" I was about to say how she'd handled the sails well while we were under way, but the captain cut me off as though disallowing my praise for her help.

"It was a good piece of work, Son." My father's compliments helped take the chill off my back. My shirt was soaked through. Anna Pearl shivered, and I took her arm and waited for the captain to lead the way up to the house.

"Thanks for the ride," she said in a low voice, smiling at me. My father nodded toward the house, indicating we should go first.

"It will be good to have you work alongside Blue on this short run across the bay," the captain said as I walked past him. "He's been on the beach so long he might have become too lubberly to manage the deck and sails alone."

Anna Pearl would not stay for dinner, though my mother entreated her to do so, and instead asked if I could give her a ride home. The captain had handed over the keys to the Buick and walked with the two of us across the backyard to where the automobile was parked.

My father closed the car door when I had positioned myself at the wheel of the Buick and maintained his grip on the window ledge. He lowered his face to look straight-on at me. I kept my eyes ahead, out beyond the windshield. Anna Pearl swung shut the passenger door, and her voice was perky when she bid the captain good evening.

"Hurry home. Your mother will have the table set by the time you get back." The captain slapped the car door, turned quickly, and walked away toward the back porch. It was just getting dusky dark, and I heard a whippoorwill as I pressed the starter button. The engine caught immediately, but I switched off the ignition.

"You hear that?"

"Yes," Anna Pearl said. "A whippoorwill makes the most lonesome sound I can imagine."

"I was actually thinking of a whippoorwill's call when we sailed past that piling at the end of the torn-down dock at the Cosper place. Remember the big pelican sitting on that piling?"

"Yes. With the yellow fuzz on its head."

"That fellow, yes. A brown pelican," I said. "To me it looked lonely. But pelicans don't talk about their loneliness."

"Talk?"

"You know," I said, "they don't have a song. Pelicans kind of grumble sometimes, but they don't sing. I was thinking if a song accompanied that sorrowful look of theirs, it would have to be sadder-sounding than even a whippoorwill's. That's all sailors would need."

"What do you mean?"

"Just that sailors tend to be a melancholy lot, and something like the baleful song of a broad-winged pelican gliding past their becalmed ships, with sails a-slatting and water everywhere but not a drop to drink . . ." I pulled my mouth into a smile, but my eyes couldn't follow, so I dropped it. The exhilaration of the sail was falling behind me, and I was left with an evening in the house with my mother and father. Dread sprang up in my stomach. I drove in silence.

"Something wrong?"

Something snapped in me, and reflexively I fired back, taking my eyes from the road to look at Anna Pearl.

"Well, what do you think? You tell me you saw my mother holding hands with a man. What would you have me do with such a prize? It's not exactly a tail-wagger, is it?"

I was as shocked at my outburst as Anna Pearl, whose eyes were wide. She situated herself tightly in the corner of the automobile seat, wedged against the door, staring at me. I looked away from her and stared straight ahead.

There was a faint yellow glow of the dashboard lights inside the car as the evening light faded from the treetops and shadows rose up from the ground. The moment was bathed in hues that both our memories would fix and seal away forever. This was the point of singularity where something between us had then and there been irrevocably altered. It was like the tiny fracture in a stone discovered by some green and growing thing, through which it pushes upward and upward until its expedition toward air and light is rewarded with a brush of fragrant wind and the sun's warm caress.

"I'm sorry, Rove."

There was the blossoming of the new: With those words from Anna Pearl, her playful skirmishes and flirtatious teasing with me were put aside like toys of childhood, and would never be taken up again. Whatever would become of our friendship would now grow in a different light.

"It's just hard, you know, like you said, to sort it all out."

"You're right." Anna Pearl relaxed and sat more comfortably on the seat. "And there's this—and I'm ashamed when I think of this—what if I'm wrong about it all, even what I saw? There may be some explanation."

"I'm not sure about that, Anna Pearl. And it's not as if I didn't consider that immediately. And repeatedly. But there are dots that seem to connect, going back a ways with my mother and father, that make the picture hard to see more than one way." I slowed the automobile and turned the big steering wheel, navigating the Buick into the Anderson driveway.

"You know, Rove," she said, her hand on the door handle as she paused before getting out of the car, "maybe it will be good for you to sail with your father to Bayou La Batre."

"At this point I don't see any damage that could come of it," I answered. "Anyway, it's not a run to New Orleans or Apalachicola. It's most of a day's sail over, by the time we get the schooner out of the river, and a day's sail back. Maybe a day or two in the repair yards. Not like twenty days at sea with my father."

Anna Pearl then asked abruptly, "If you go off to the war, can you admit that you're using the navy to help you run away?" Anna Pearl still had not opened her door, but looked over her shoulder toward the front door of her house, as if expecting her mother to walk out onto the gallery and wave her inside.

"Sure, I can admit that. It's not a new thing for men to do." I smiled when Anna Pearl lifted her eyebrows. "All right, for *young* men. Anyway, it's an escape with pay, with a bunk and a meal. Plus, there's at least a little honor in running away to fight for your country."

Anna Pearl looked toward her front door again, then back at me. "Rove, I really must go inside. I know you'll sail early in the morning. I do hope something good comes of this trip."

"So do I, and I think there's about as much chance of that as there is that it will not."

Anna Pearl leaned across the seat, and this time I knew she was going to kiss me. I moved toward her and closed my eyes when her lips touched mine. Her mouth was damp and warm and the touch of her lips was as soft as the scent of summer rain. Our kiss, this time, seemed to me as easy and natural as a hug or a pat on the shoulder, but my heart still raced, and burned warm in my chest, and my thoughts wheeled and turned and rose up high above the Buick, soaring in feathered flight like a seabird over the morning waves.

nna Pearl Anderson had just kissed me. She had kissed me once before, and that's the right way to say it, *she* kissed *me*. Not altogether unlike saying that she slapped me. This time *we* kissed. I don't know how the subtle signal is passed between two people, or how you could identify who has taken the split-second advantage and initiated a kiss, but the distinction is so fine when a kiss is *we*, and not *she* or *he*, that it's almost a perfect display of mutual and simultaneous assent between two people.

A kiss is a kiss, but, like the Great Way to God at its mystical best, what a kiss is cannot be spoken of.

Nor can a sixteen-year-old boy speak coherently and with honesty of encountering his mother that first time after coming to doubt her faithfulness to his father.

You can talk about it. You could write about it. But you could no sooner have those jots and tittles on a page convey the twisting in your guts and the blunt pain in your mind than you can tell someone what a strawberry tastes like. Ordinarily, I'd say pain is initiated in a nerve ending and read by the mind, and echoed back to the nerves. But this blow arose in my mind, was sustained in my mind, and caused my mind to doubt much of what, up to then, it had named and held holy.

You just know that something hurts in the part of you that knows, or, here, *thought* it knew. You can't point for the doctor and show him where it hurts. It's free-floating and pervasive. Would that it had locus, for then, by measures precise and heroic the injured part could be excised, or at some point of desperation, ripped out, shaken loose, and thrown over the fence.

When an adolescent boy learns his mother has violated the trust of his father, and his trust, and his trust in the idea of what a mother is, the bedrock foundation is *presto change-o* transmogrified into shapeless, shifting sand, as dangerous as the grit in a mummy's mouth. All because she took into each of her hands the hands of a man, not your father, and held them with tenderness, and held his eyes with tenderness in a room where she thought no one else would see.

It would take me some time to arise and walk from this knowledge. And, like a well-erased chalkboard with its dusty white swirls and clouds, there'd still be marks to deal with. The *pentimento* would grow by layers, the first of them applied that night at the supper Mother cooked in my honor for coming back home to her after a long week of nights camped on my sloop.

The table was set. My father sat at the head and I to his side. Everything seemed to me moving in slow motion. I saw close-ups of my mother's hands setting down a heaping plate of cornmeal-battered fried okra. I saw my father's eyes watching her move about the kitchen, with my knees scissoring back and forth underneath the table. No one spoke. Mother was fidgety, making three trips to the stove for two dishes, not setting the salt and pepper shakers on the table.

"Oh, what was that again?" she asked the second time my father mentioned he'd not ever seen the dress she was wearing.

Did my mother think that Anna Pearl had told me what she saw? Did she think that I would confront her? *Never.* Did she worry that the captain would divine the nature of her anxiety? She dropped a plate of corn bread, between the stove and the table, and the heavy china plate broke into two pieces and corn bread scattered over the floor.

"Lillian, what the hell is wrong with you this evening?" My father's voice erupted before, even, the pieces of the plate had come to a full rest. "You are behaving like a sailor who's been in the captain's rum!"

"Oh, Dominus, can you not forgive a mother's nerves?"

She began sobbing, and I had never seen her come to tears like that in a back-and-forth with my father. She put her face into her hands, still standing over the mess on the kitchen floor. "I have not seen my son in a week."

My father got up and left the room. To his credit, for

once he had not joined the skirmish. I'd never seen him just up and leave like that, with nothing to say. And I believed it was his wartime mission to overhaul his ship that took precedence. In this instance, I might have wanted to excuse myself from my mother's presence, but I did not follow the captain.

When my mother raised her face from her palms, when she had blinked away the blur, when her reddened eyes met my own, she knew in an instant that I knew what Anna Pearl had seen, and she turned her back and lowered her head and her hair fell forward over her trembling shoulders.

I kept my seat at the table, my hands on my knees, and they were still rocking back and forth. I did not move to stand. My mother lifted her head and tilted it back with a shake, and her pretty hair was shining as it fell back into place, and she walked out of the kitchen without looking back at me.

I see her going now as clearly as I saw her then.

When my father awakened me at 4 a.m. on the morning of December 20, 1941, the first thing I heard was rain on the roof. The captain opened the door to my bedroom and said, not loudly, "It's four. We'll be leaving in thirty minutes."

I rolled over and put my feet on the floor, feeling the cold pine planks, and switched on the lamp on my bedside table. The low-wattage bulb spilled dim yellow light into the room. I yawned and found myself thinking that if my father were a carpenter, and this were a day when the son would join him to work, the rain would likely send us back to bed. It would take a ruckus of a storm to keep a sailor in bed and his ship in port, and rainfall, even heavy and blowing sideways, would never stop Dominus MacNee, nor would most fully founded storms for that matter.

By the time I was dressed and had collected some clothes and stuffed them into my grip and made it into the kitchen, the captain was wrapping up the last of some cold biscuits and salt pork. He took two apples from the bowl on the counter and shoved one into each of his front jacket pockets, then picked two more and tossed them to me.

The captain's heavy canvas duffel bag was leaning against the wall beside the back door. I knew that my mother had not been back in the kitchen since walking out of it the night before. There was a foreboding silence in the kitchen, almost like an eerie echo of her exit. The captain had nothing to say into the quiet. Dominus MacNee was not a talkative man in the mornings, especially when he was preparing to sail. But mostly, it was my father's eyes that refused to speak to me. He seemed to purposefully avoid looking at me, and what I could see of the soft brown irises and black pupils seemed withdrawn into the shadows of an interior landscape of lost or abandoned purpose.

The captain reached for the aluminum coffeepot, hot on a low blue gas flame on the stove's front eye. He poured a cup, and the black brew smelled good to me, though I did not ask for a cup. The coffee looked like some magic elixir flowing into the heavy ceramic mug, the same one my father had taken with him to the *Mary Foster* at his daybreak departures for as long as I could remember. Once bright white, the cup's glaze was now yellowed and crazed, stained dark brown around its lip.

I knew that my father had not poured his cup full, that he'd add nothing to it, and that this was our signal to grab our grips and head out the back door of the kitchen to the waiting truck. The captain said nothing nor gestured to me, only took up his canvas duffel. His big fingers were curled into the coffee cup's mansized handle, and he stood waiting for me to open the door.

It was dark outside. Roosting birds had not yet begun to stir and the rain was now slowed to a soft drizzle, muting the gentle sweep of the wind in the high branches of the sugar pines. The squat magnolias, like sleeping gnomes, were untouched by the dawn breeze, and their broad waxy leaves were still as a widow's hands in church, and neither poet nor prophet would have missed the omen.

We were soon on the road and in high gear, and I rode in the company of ideas heavy enough to cup my own hands around, uncertainties enough to stir my blood, and silence deep enough for a Protestant baptism.

It should have been a three-day sail. A day over, a day in the yards for miscellaneous repairs my father had put off until just this downtime, and a day's sail back across the bay and into Fish River to the anchorage at Farragut's Turn. But who could have known that this voyage would sail me down years, toss me through sleepless nights, and run me aground on an emotional shoal beset with hazards of guilt and memory and fear? I'm not sure that the *Mary Foster* will ever close her logbook entry on that voyage.

We *stopped for Blue* at his cottage on North School Street. He came out to the truck with a large canvas bag that had big looping handles of leather and tossed it into the back of the truck underneath the tarpaulin. It was raining steadily again, though not hard, and there was no wind. Blue bounced into the seat beside me before I'd had time to slide to the middle to make room for him, and I wound up being squashed against his side and shoved over.

"Sorry, lad," he apologized, shaking the rain from his hands, wiping his palms on his knees. "I'm 240 pounds of pure sugar, and this rain would soon melt me down. 'Twould not be a pretty sight."

If my father and I were quiet, Blue was noisy. His enthusiasm was almost like a child's, and I wondered how he would behave on Christmas morning next week. He lived alone, but I believed I'd find a decorated tree in his tiny house. In his merriment he seemed oblivious to the outbreak of war, and he did not once mention the bombing in Hawaii.

The thin odor of motor oil and gasoline fumes and the scent of the captain's coffee blended in the cab of the truck. Blue leaned forward and looked over at my father. "How does yer boat go with soppy wet sails? She'll still lay her mark before day's end, aye Skipper?"

My father did not take his eyes off the windshield in front of him. "Unless I drive her onto the oyster shoals," he said, the first thing from his mouth since he'd announced my wake-up call.

"And if ye do that, I'll take extra pay."

Blue rattled on about this and that thing of no consequence without much pause. Not that my father or I looked for an opening where we might add to his monologue. I did not know Blue well and had not spent much time in his company, but still was surprised to find him so garrulous. And it occurred to me that what I'd at first interpreted as gaiety began to sound like nervous chatter, and I wondered when he had last sailed. Of late I had only seen him stevedoring on the Big Pier, though I knew he'd decked before on the *Mary Foster*.

By the time we parked the truck in the clearing adjacent to the riverbank on the east side of Fish River at Farragut's Turn, the rain had stopped and the sky was losing the dimness of dawn, and the sun's full light behind the cloud cover was swirled into patterns and shades of white and gray and black.

"There's wind in them clouds, Skipper," said Blue, his voice booming over his shoulder as he worked the lines at the bow of the *Mary Foster*.

"Precisely what a schooner requires to do her business," said my father.

"Its business ain't ever to turn over, is it, sir?" Blue was still facing forward and appeared to be cautiously exploring this topic.

My father stopped and raised up from the stern cleat, the two-cylinder diesel engine thumping a slow bass count down in the belly of the ship, little chugging splashes coming from the stern as the exhaust stroke pumped its cooling water overboard. He studied Blue's back, then glanced at me. There was no smile on his lips, but there was mischief dancing in his eyes, and the brown of them began to shine.

"No, it's when she's playing that she lays down her rail and ships a bit of water over the decks," my father said. "And she does love to play in this December air. Santa Claus is coming, you know."

Blue stood up straight from faking down a dock line on deck, dropped the end of the line on top of the coil, and turned around. "And I am still a wee boy at heart, Skipper. I'll be wanting to see jolly old Mister Whiskers on Christmas morning," he said, then added with emphasis, "Sir, please and thank ye."

I had my Christmas right then, for the captain, my father, broke loose with a great belly laugh. There could not have been a thing in a stack of Sears & Roebuck catalogs to the ceiling that could have been a better gift than watching my father's head rock back and his shoulders shake with laughter. It was not merely heard and seen, I felt it. The captain might just as well have wrapped his arms around me and rubbed his whiskered cheek on mine.

The skies over Mobile Bay were boiling, odd colors: a bruised-looking yellow and black. Lightning ripped through the mess overhead as my father ordered me out of the *Mary Foster*'s cabin and onto the deck. I had gone below to study the chart of this portion of the bay. My father had only joked to Blue about grounding on the oyster reefs, and now that possibility lay as a real danger.

We had no sooner sailed out of Weeks Bay, through the pass known as Big Mouth, and into the wider waters of the bay than the weather deteriorated quickly into a full gale. That the captain of the *Mary Foster* had not anticipated the storm was unusual. I had known times when my father had foreseen bad weather even before the glass began to register the falling pressure.

Other skippers had been known to come around Magnolia Bayhouse on the pretense of making a casual visit, but had been announced by my grandmother, "Dominus, someone's here for a weather forecast." She'd winked at me and added when Captain Ray Parmley had once strolled onto our back porch, "Cap'n Ray's looking for wind and tides for next June, Dominus. And whether or not he'll be caught smuggling in his rum from Havana."

When I had yelled over the screech of the wind that I was going to have a look at the charts, my father had been so busy managing the pitch and yaw of the twisting vessel, running as she was before a northwest blow over her stern, that he had not said a word, only looked over the bowsprit like he was trying to burn a clear passage to calmer waters.

The fact that we were running downwind was another telltale sign for me that the captain was distracted and his senses dulled. He had not kept his eye on the compass and had brought the *Mary Foster* too far north into the shallow waters along the western shore just south of Fowl River. So now we were forced to sail almost due south ahead of a wildly building wind that cut its eye left or right too quickly for the captain to make smooth adjustments to the helm, and there was a threat of making an accidental jibe that, in this weather, could easily rip down a mast.

When I climbed out of the companionway and slid the hatch back into place, I saw that Blue was on the foredeck, fighting his way forward on the madly rolling deck.

As is so often the case on a ship battling a storm, when one thing goes wrong, another seems to follow, and if those dominoes keep falling, you find a ship that is in great peril. The captain had ordered Blue to go forward. The starboard jib sheet had parted, and the wild flapping of the sail had snatched the port sheet out from around the winch and off the cleat, and the headsail was snapping and popping out of control in the strong wind, which pulverized the rain and turned it into a fine spray blown sideways.

The wind switched directions so rapidly that the mainsail was almost backwinded and the boom gave a heave upward, its warning, like a rattler about to strike, that if you don't snatch back your control, it will in the next moment slam the boom across to the other side and try to snap your mainmast like a dry twig. Dominus MacNee saw it coming and cried in a fierce and remarkably loud voice, "Jibe, ho!"

What happened next, I could not believe. In retrospect, I could only add this bizarre event to a string of miscues from the captain since embarking on this sail. I think my father had let himself see, finally, what had been peering at him from the shadows for so long: His Lillian had found another man. I do believe that my mother's face was on that day in south Mobile Bay blinding my father, grounding his sailor's will and wisdom.

The captain quickly raised his right arm in an instinctive gesture as if to ward off the swing of the boom, an action as ill-fated as trying to raise your hands to fend off a bullet from a gun fired at you point-blank. I watched, frozen in that curious way when the mind pours out time as sap from its great wounded trunk into a cold Vermont morning, and it thickens and pearls and stops still. My father's arm went up—and I would always remember seeing, as his billowing sleeve slid down his wrist, the gold watch my mother had given to the captain on his birthday three years ago.

I had seen him wear it for only about a month after getting it, and then it had come to rest on the corner of his desk, slipped onto the outstretched arm of a bronze figurine, a sailor pointing out to sea. Odd, I would later think, how my eye went to that watch. Did I wish to avoid my father's eyes?

When the 250-pound boom swung with the speed and ease of a hickory bat in the hands of a home run hitter, there could be only one outcome for anything standing in that furious arc: It would be shattered like hollow ceramic. The captain's entire upper torso was whipped into the air and he was flung instantly overboard into the brown froth as his son and the Irishman watched without even time to cry out or raise a hand.

I'm not sure what prevented me from instinctively jumping into the water in a crazed effort to save my father, though I knew by the limp composure of his body upon impact, like an oversized rag doll, that the bones in his back and neck and chest were crushed and that he was dead. Instead, I cried out for Blue to hang on as I sprang to the ship's wheel. But it was spinning like a drive gear in a full-throttle machine. I could only brace my thigh against the cockpit seat for balance, my hands up like a bandit's target, waiting to grab onto the wheel when it ceased to turn.

The fact that the helm was free of all resistance except the push of dark water against rudder, and that the *Mary*

Foster had found her own sympathetic response to the mad pivot of bow and stern and the roll of the hull in the trough between whitecapped swells, was probably what saved the mainmast from toppling onto the deck in a mess of lines and canvas.

With her bow having come up on the eye of the wind, and the sails luffing and snapping like small shot being fired from several weapons, the helm stopped spinning and I took hold of it, the vessel now in noisy irons. Blue had somehow remained on deck, still on his feet even, wide-legged and crouching.

"Come take the wheel," I screamed, and in a series of bounding, surefooted leaps, the big man was in the cockpit and had hold of the helm. He didn't ask a thing, his hard gaze only briefly shifting over his shoulder in the direction of where my father had been knocked into the water. There was not a chance the captain would be seen again until his body might be found when the storm abated.

"I'm going on the foredeck to backwind the jib," I yelled, "and if I can do it, you quickly spin the wheel to bring her to the wind!"

And I turned and quick-footed along the side deck toward the bow. I went straight for the port jib sheet, my arms up to prevent my face from being stung by its lashing. The very end of the line was over the side, trailing in the water, but a loop of it was twisting and whipping at me, and the three-quarter-inch line struck me on the ear with such force it almost knocked me down.

I grabbed the loop of jib sheet and hauled the line back

aboard, coiling it in my left hand. It was luck, really, that came to the fore so that when I lunged for the flapping sail, my hand caught hold of the clew of the jib. I gripped that corner of the triangular canvas and held on with more force than I would have believed of myself, so that it wasn't ripped from my grasp when I presented the sail broadside to the wind, pulled taut in front of my body.

As soon as the bow began to respond, moving off the wind, I knew I had only a few seconds before the power of the wind in the sail would rip the jib from my hand, and I moved immediately to cleat off the sheet, letting go the clew and holding my small advantage with the line in my hand. There was a deck cleat three steps away, and I charged for it, bent, and made my figure eight over the ears of the cleat in less than three seconds. The full force of the wind now found purchase in the triangle of canvas and spun the bow hard and fast downwind.

"Now, Blue! Now! Bring her about!" I screamed.

It did not matter that the boat could not be steered up-wind, or that Blue understand that. All I needed of him was for him to spin the helm. And Blue did that at precisely the right time.

Before either of us could let out a breath, the ship was hove to, heeled at fifteen degrees, and stalled with her port side presented to the wind. The effect was miraculous. The ship felt set in iron, albeit with a howling wind putting up a fierce protest.

"Keep the helm hard over, Blue!" I yelled, and without an instant's pause I freed the upside-down skiff from its chocks on the foredeck and heaved it into the water with a splash. I landed in the middle of the skiff before it had settled on the waves and unstrapped the oars, set one in each oarlock, and dug into the froth with them both in such a way as to spin the small craft so that I was headed in the direction where my father's body might be floating.

I was crying now, and keening and moaning into the wind, and I stroked the oars like a Norse warrior. I knew this was foolish and could only hope that Blue would not dive into the torn water to join me and try to help me in my futile efforts and drown for his deed. The Irishman did not, only stood sculpted to the helm so that when I, after thirty minutes of frantic rowing, gave up and grew quiet and returned to the *Mary Foster*, Blue had not moved, nor did he look in my direction.

I let the skiff bang into the hull on the leeward side, and in the windshadow was able to heft myself aboard with the bow painter in my hand. I hauled the heavy skiff onto the foredeck like it was a toy, my mind unaware of the weight of the boat, the veins in my muscles pouring adrenaline.

When I had quickly secured the skiff into its chocks, I turned and sat down on the forward cabin roof and put my face in my hands and without so much as a flicker of thought, said aloud: "The Lord is my shepherd, I shall not want. He makes me to lie down in green pastures. He restores my soul. He leads me beside the peaceful waters for his name's sake. Yea, though I walk through the valley of the shadow of death I will fear no evil. Thou art with me." I shook my head and lifted my face to the storm over my head, my eyes alight, clear, and piercing the roiling gray clouds. "Thou art with me and I will fear no evil."

And my voice disappeared from my tongue as the wet breath of the wind churned the air in front of my face, and yet it did not mock my loss, only shuddered and heaved and sighed as though the wind itself did feel the grief, and was frustrated that it had no consolation to give this boy.

Fishermen *from Bayou* La Batre found his body before the week was out, and his funeral mass was preached by Father John Brown at Sacred Heart's bayside chapel according to the wishes of Dominus MacNee. It was a prodigal son's Catholic homecoming. The captain had lain in state in an oak casket in the very same spot beneath the mantel in the parlor where my grandmother took her leave of this world, there in front of the fireplace, watched over by all those dusty photos of kinfolks.

And now the sepia tint of the photos on the mantel seemed gathered like some melancholy pigment, its sadness water-brushed over the whole of the town. Reddened eyes blinked wide with wonder and disbelief that Captain MacNee could have made such a lubberly mistake, that he could be killed by a pole swung by the wind.

Blue had stirred passions about town with the skill of a politician, and it was not long until the winds of gossip and speculation fixed in an oblique manner the blame for Father's death on my mother.

"If the captain'd been a railroad man with a woman like that, he'd a laid out on the tracks and waited his neck for the through-train express." And other versions like it were heard from the barbershop to the hardware store, in church and on the Big Pier. When my mother left town, I half expected the talk to hit the *Fairhope Courier*.

Blue had driven the captain's flatbed Ford from Farragut's to Magnolia Bayhouse that miserable day, and the rain muted the landscape and presented it in soft gray washes like an Oriental painting. The sail back across the bay and up the river had been accomplished by some sleight of hand. Blue and I might have been the last two hands on a ghost ship, lacking animation and any light in our eyes. I was so lost by the time we arrived home that Blue had opened the passenger door for me and stood back while my feet went down for miles to the shell drive by the big azaleas. He'd come to a stop out back of our house in just the same place my father always parked.

I asked Blue to come inside with me, and he'd put his big hand on my shoulder in answer. Thinking back, it now seems odd to me that I didn't have him drive himself home first so that I alone would meet my mother with the awful news.

That day for me, however, was not marked by discernment of what was a right and fitting thing to do. Blue kept his hand clamped onto my shoulder as we walked across

the yard to the back door of the house, and he walked behind me down the hall and into my father's study.

We found Josef Unruh seated at my father's desk.

My surprise was nothing more than a mutter caught in
my throat and quickly devolved to unspoken anger. But
what was back of my anger was so intensely alight in my
eyes that Blue saw it and himself flashed fury like a torch
put to a fat fuse running into a bundle of red dynamite
sticks.

Then it was I who put my hand on his shoulder and
grabbed his wide biceps. His whole body telegraphed a
killing rage, and Blue, I do believe, would have mauled the
German on the spot if my mother had not walked in with
a pot of tea and two cups on a silver platter with linen
napkins.

That was when the locus of my anger shifted.

I took one look at my mother, who certainly had not
expected visitors, and least of all her son and a giant Irishman bringing bad news. And when I spoke, the words
might have been propelled with the full force of the back
of my hand. "Mother, he's dead. My father is dead. Will
you ask this man to leave?"

All of us had then gone wooden and voiceless until
Mother made as if to come to me, but fell there on the
floor in a heap. It was a scene painted heavy with the darker
pigments of souls slipping into the keeping shadows.

"Don't touch my mother," I said as Josef Unruh arose,
quick-stepped around the desk, and bent to see about her.

"If ye don't leave now, I'll sure and for certain kill ye, man," Blue said in a voice far too calm to match the moment and the knot in his jaw, hard as the heart of a fallen pine. Anger swelled in the craw of the big Irishman, and he took two steps in the direction of Josef Unruh. When it looked like the two men would tangle then and there, I looked up from my mother and said quietly, "Leave us. Please, Blue. Both of you go."

The German left first, and Blue waited back to make sure I was all right, that my mother would come around. When she stirred and her eyes fluttered open, Blue took his leave without so much as a word. His talk was saved for the town.

From the get-go, my mother was not exactly convincing in her role as grieving widow. Her collapse on the floor when I told her Father was dead was the only break in her guarded emotional stance. Before sunset the next day, her back was straight and her lips thin and tight behind all the talk.

Then, after the funeral, Blue led a vigilante gang to the German's door in the middle of the night and offered Josef Unruh the choice of his life in some other place, or his death in Fairhope. The accused man took a panel truck loaded with his things and left town just at sunset two days before Christmas.

People turned their talk to what my mother might do. She could have gone to Eucharist at Saint James', perhaps, and at the place in the service for prayers of the people, Miss Lillian could have stood and raised her chin and lifted her voice toward the altar and asked for forgiveness for the busybody rumormongers. "Josef Unruh stopped by Magnolia Bayhouse in broad daylight, a visit from a friend. May the Lord have mercy on your accusing souls."

And if one, or a chorus, had responded in the vehement manner of accusing souls: *But Josef Unruh and Dominus MacNee rolled in the dirt like mongrel dogs prowling and scrapping after a bitch in heat,* Lillian MacNee could have said, "The only two-legged dogs in this town are wagging their tongues because their tails are tucked so tightly."

And she had maintained to me, while lifting her suitcase and laying a hand to the back of Julian's shoulder to urge him into the open door of the automobile, that she'd had quite enough of the talk, and that since she was free to leave, leave she would. She charged me with "keeping up the place." She said she knew I would be all right until she came back to Alabama.

"And what about Julian, Mother?" Julian was crying. I know he wanted me to stop her from taking him, a thing I would not do. I was not capable of taking my brother to raise, could not then be his keeper. I could not look straight at Julian, nor at my mother, and so watched a centipede negotiate the sun-bleached shells at my feet.

"We have heard so many times on Sunday mornings, Rove, that knowing the truth will set us free. And when you get to the truth, I hope you find the freedom to love me again." She stepped up to me and patted my cheek in just the same gentle way Granny Wooten would. There was no point in my telling Mother that I believed a week's gossip was only thin icing on a cake that had been baking for months.

And I can say that my mother never once offered to reconcile her departure from Magnolia Bayhouse and Fairhope. Down the years, her first and final words on the matter were those she said to me as she closed her car door to leave: "Christmas does not have to be spoiled. If we go now, Santa Claus will find Julian in a sweet bed at my sister's house." With only suitcases and Julian, Mother left Fairhope in the Buick, and I would not see her again for almost nine years.

I drove to *Anna Pearl's* house in my father's flatbed. She would not be expecting me, couldn't have known my mother had left. I really had no idea what I was doing, traveling in something like a dream where I could see myself driving. I would play it by ear. I was not even out of the Ford when Anna Pearl snatched open the driver's-side door and leaned into the truck and kissed me without a word.

"I knew you'd come," she said, stepping back to look me up and down as I got out of the car. She put her hands on her hips. I stood there like a schoolboy. Anna Pearl's hair tumbled around her shoulders, and her eyes and mouth and figure were so gloriously rendered on the canvas of my mind that she erased all the other thoughts in my head.

I fumbled for something to say and remembered that I'd come to see if she wanted to ride with me to Magnolia Springs and see the giant tree that would come to be known as Inspiration

Oak. I blurted out that there would be a harvest moon and it would be perfect light for looking at a tree.

"Oh," she said, "I love it when the moon takes over the sky from brother sun. Of course, I'd love to go. I've heard of that tree, but I've never been to see it. Let me get my sweater."

She came out with an apple for each of us, and we ate them as we drove south toward Fish River, and just across it to the farmer's field where the old oak tree grew. There wasn't as much light as we'd imagined, and Anna Pearl snagged her dress crossing the barbed-wire fence in the dark. I led the way, and we found our way through the tall grass, chattering softly, just above whispering. We were trespassing on private property. We kept our eyes down mostly, watching our step.

Finally I stopped and stepped to the side, taking Anna Pearl's elbow and guiding her around a low-hanging branch that swooped down toward us off the giant trunk like the neck of a curious brontosaurus. When we were underneath the canopy of the other branches, shielded from above, and unable any longer to see the night sky, Anna Pearl went completely silent and stood still as a woman in prayer. Far off toward the river an owl called, but softly, and soon was quiet. I stood beside her, could feel the brush and tickle of the hair on our arms, could smell her soap and shampoo and powdered skin. I could have been on the moon, with no trees at all: This girl at my side was the only other thing in existence at that moment.

I have no idea where it came from, but I looked at Anna Pearl, at her face brushed by the moon's silver light, and asked if she'd go sailing with me the next day. I thought she was going to laugh at me, and was completely surprised when she turned in front of me, took both my hands, and tugged me down with her onto the leaves.

Today *Anna Pearl* and I sailed in Mobile Bay. Warm sun. Light southern winds. We dropped the anchor, doused the sails, and talked about my enlisting in the navy. The subject seemed to rile her, and she said she could easily see that I'd want to leave town, and if I couldn't think of a good reason to stay around Fairhope, then I should just leave. Now, if that's all decided, she said, then I'll go swimming. Without another word she stripped to her underclothes and dove over the side of the *Sea Bird* into the frigid water.

I'd swum in cold water plenty of times, but seeing her splashing out there gave me the shivers. I stayed aboard and watched her, and was pretty soon thinking I'd never seen dolphins at play or anything in the water that looked so lovely. She swam near the boat, and the water was unusually clear. My heart beat fast, and I thought my mind would just fade to white.

Would you stop ogling the girl in the water and get in the water, too? Anna Pearl always speaks directly. Then she threatened to swim to shore if I didn't come in the water. And I knew she meant it. So I stripped to my underwear and splashed in beside her. She wrestled me under. Later, out of breath and hanging on the gunwale of my boat, kicking our legs in the chilly water, she told me if I was leaving not to think that she would wait around for me to come home.

It was now the end of January. The frigid Gulf of Mexico lay ahead of the rise and fall of the *Sea Bird*'s bowsprit. Two weeks ago I had shut the door to my bedroom at Magnolia Bayhouse, walked out the back door, and pulled it closed and locked it.

Anna Pearl had come to the house with me after our sail, and when I tried to kiss her as we stood looking at family pictures on the wall in the hallway, she put her fingers on my lips. It was the lightest touch I've ever known, and yet an omen, like a light breeze from the east. "And when the wind is from the east, 'tis good for neither man nor beast," I'd heard the captain sing a hundred times, that old sailor's refrain. I watched as Anna Pearl's eyes grew red and wet, and tears spilled onto her cheeks. Neither of us said a word, and she had left by the back door while I still stood in the hallway. It was my mother's beautiful eyes that I looked into there on the wall as I tried to settle the moment in my head.

The next day I went to the post office and

mailed a letter to my mother at her sister's address in Mississippi. In it I told her the house was closed up and the windows shuttered, and that she might write to Father Brown before coming home and ask him to open the place up and let it breathe out its musty smells for a few days before she and Julian got there.

Lillian MacNee never came back to Fairhope, and a genteel decay settled on the cottage, and the grounds went wild and green and Julian sank ten thousand dollars into the place when he later got married and bought it from our mother.

When I sailed out of Fly Creek, and out of Mobile Bay, I had a vague idea to sail west toward New Orleans, maybe find work on the docks where my father had traded. I managed the tiller, holding my course with the north wind fresh on my starboard quarter, the *Sea Bird* heeling to her best lines and finding every knot of speed she was allowed.

In those easy moments sailing under the winter sun, it occurred to me that it was the face of the captain at the center of the numbness that swirled and tingled in me, though Anna Pearl was spinning there on the periphery. My hope of relief lay at the eye of this thing, and seeking work among men who had known him would put me in the middle of the hurt. And the hurt had surprised me, springing unexpected from my psyche like a determined tendril from a scuppernong vine, curling toward the light, a brightness issuing from forgiveness. It's easier to reconcile a bad story if you know the sense behind its first line.

Belief flickered in my mind and grew over the years that the captain saw his Lillian slip past that moment when all husbands or wives can say, simply, aloud or to one's self, *no. Yes* is a single moment's willingness extended to finality, like a step into the air above a precipice.

There is no coming back. Everything changes. Anger and grief get soaked raw and bleeding in whiskey, and whores nurse the maligned heart. I could see it.

I even believed I could see Granny Wooten's passing as the spike upon which hung the whole of my mother's weakness. Absent the guidance, and loaded with sadness, Lillian MacNee set the little nail and tap-tapped, hardly attendant to the deed. I could account for the captain's misaligned malice finding its way to me if I remember the time that Julian kicked Elberta off the porch at Magnolia Bayhouse. When I asked him why he did that, he told me that the chain kept jumping off his bicycle.

When a storm bunched up on the horizon, quickly, I fought down an unexpected chill that crept up my spine, knowing it had nothing to do with the wind. Maybe I was not yet ready for another storm, for the ghosts that would scud by me on the howl. Maybe I should turn back. There was such an exhortation to turn my boat around from back there in the captain's study, when Emerson spoke from the pages of his book of essays, saying, ". . . let us not rove; let us sit at home with the cause."

And the sense of Emerson's entreaty to not step away from our lot in life is that we cannot escape its impact, anyway. "I pack my trunk," he wrote, "embrace my friends, embark on the sea, and at last wake up in Naples, and there beside me is the stern fact, the sad self, unrelenting, identical, that I fled from. . . . My giant goes with me wherever I go."

So clear and tempting was the voice of Emerson in my head that I was all but ready to put the tiller hard over and bring the *Sea Bird* around. But the night was coming on soon, and I thought to anchor out at least until morning. My charts showed a little north shore cove just inside the pass at Petit Bois island in the Mississippi Sound. There was good wind from the northwest, and I soon brought the tip of Petit Bois into sight. As soon as I sailed into the cove there, I spotted the camp of Walter Anderson.

The artist waved me into the little harbor and invited me to stay, if I would camp aboard my boat and not pester him while he sketched and painted. He made it clear that I was to enjoy his company only upon invitation.

"And, when I sail on to Ocean Springs," he said, "—which departing I will not clear with you, it could be tonight or in a month—you may not follow. You are on your own, boy."

"I am on my own," I had replied, the words coming up from the core of me, ringing with the finality of a judge's pronouncement of sentence.

The artist softened with the news of the death of my father, and our two weeks together had gone easily for us both, and I had enjoyed the solitary nights on my boat, the black winter sky littered with a million stars. Each night I slept more soundly. The artist's voice from our daytime repartee sang back to me in the darkness, his renderings of line and form and light and shadow like a tone poem on a Victrola. He had told me on a walk around the western end of the island how he wished he could join the orange-beaked royal terns on the wind at twilight, how bending wings into that magical hour would be to sail right into heaven's gate.

I'd turned into my rack even earlier than usual that night, finding sleep ready and waiting for me on my thin pillow. I had fallen into a dream as easily as drinking down a glass of cold, sweet water on a summer's day. The dream images ran on and off the stage of my groggy mind, but no story line took hold. When I felt the thump against the hull, at first I thought that my anchor had dragged, that my keel had struck the sandy bottom on the lee shore of the cove cut into the north side of this barrier island. When *Sea Bird* tipped heavily to starboard, I fumbled through my sleeping mind to come awake and, opening my eyes, swung my feet to the cabin sole and reached for my trousers. I feared I'd drifted aground in the cove. I poked my head out of the companionway.

It was the artist. He had swum to my boat, and in a rough whisper said, "Come on deck. Look! There's a waterspout skirting the island." I tripped on the ladder coming out of the companionway and banged my shin on the bottom pinboard I'd left in to keep back some of the night's chill from inside my boat.

"Shhh," he said. "You'll make it fly away." This artist from Mississippi was a pure delight, something like a glimpse at redemption for me.

The artist dragged himself on board and, up on cat feet, stepped along the deck to the bow. In the diffuse light of a half moon, he looked like he might have escaped from my dreams. He was wearing long johns, which clung to him dripping wet. He paid no mind to the cold night air, but the sight of him made me shiver. I joined the soaking artist on the bow. He stepped out onto the bowsprit, hanging on to the jib stay. He began speaking, but quiet, like a man in church.

"Ah, look there. Just look! It would be an affront to God to reach for a pen and paper now. Do you think so?"

Walter Anderson looked at me, then away, turning his face rapidly back to the swirling funnel whipping its gauzy tail over the water not three hundred yards away. A great loud swish and low thrum filled the air. Phosphorus was being sucked up into the watery spray, and it looked like the column of mist was dipped into the dust of those million stars. The two of us might have been watching the passing of Jesus. Neither of us seemed to mind the frosted wind on our necks.

"Old-timers say they're easy to break apart," Walter Anderson whispered. "They say a waterspout is the ghost of a tornado, like a spectral appearance of the moaning vortex that has not long since ripped lives from this earth."

He motioned for me to come farther. I took a step and was right beside the artist, who tonight had a palpable presence that emanated from his body, and I could feel it like a mother's nudge in a warm kitchen with tea cakes baking in the oven.

"I met an old shrimper in Biloxi who told me a waterspout in a night when the moon is full portends death. Someone well known by the watcher will die within a fortnight." The painter looked at me. "Son of a sailor, what do you know about these omens?"

"I've heard of waterspouts at night," I said, my voice low, my eyes on the man before me. "This is the first I've seen."

Walter Anderson put his hand on my shoulder and looked straight into my eyes, and I was struck with a feeling of wonder and awe for the audacity of this man, not the spinning mist, caught as I was in those eyes, eyes that saw what I could not—birds as sweeps and swirls of line, trees as patterned mosaics. Then the artist turned back to look again at the serpentine wraith, moving away to the east.

I was quiet for a moment. "My father said to me once that a sound like the boom of a cannon could drop a night spout right from the sky and make it fall like silver rain on troubled waves."

The artist moved his hand from my shoulder. "I believe him, boy," he said, shaking his head. "Such terrors in the heart, and yet so terribly fragile."

And I felt in the thump of my own heart a good deep resonance, freeborn like thunder, and thought it refuge enough against my fears, sufficient haven for my dreams.

Acknowledgments

Word is, *a writer's working* life is a solitary occupation. It's true that only my fingers poke these lettered keys, and that I can't make a good sentence if I'm distracted by ringing bells and barking dogs and a party going on over my shoulder. So I hole up. I sequester myself in a room filled with keepsakes and talismans sure to charm the muse, a room with a pleasant view out the window down a rolling grassy hillside dotted with oaks and pines and the handsomest dogwood I've ever seen. My private sanctuary for writing.

I think of the *Paris Review* "Writers at Work" series, and of reading E. B. White's piece there. He said he loved the distraction of children, and placed his writing desk in the central foyer of his farmhouse so at that busy crossroad he'd soon get a tug on the sleeve and be asked out to the barn to see this or that mystery. It worked for him.

I get my writing done, however, all alone.

But do I?

Of course not. Matter of fact, there's always

this list of people to acknowledge, for the record, who helped my novel into the world. Take down any book from your shelf, and you'll see that most writers take a page or two at the front of their books to say thank you for the help they got. Everything from moral support and friend-ship to story ideas and editing.

I always forget to name someone who's been important to me in my job as a writer. Like Frank Turner Hollon, who has mentioned my name on the acknowledgments page in all five of his books. So, I'm getting a new dog, a playmate for Cormac, and I'm naming it Frank. Plus giv-ing him this entire paragraph, short though it is, as an act of contrition for my forgetfulness. How could I fail to mention a writer who gave me the title for the anthology series I edit, *Stories from the Blue Moon Café*?

Then, there are all the other people I want to thank:

There's my fine editor, Johanna Bowman, and all the rest of the gang at Random House and Ballantine, Gina Centrello, Nancy Miller, Kim Hovey, Cindy Murray, Allison Dickens, Anthony Ziccardi, and Steven Wallace, all of whom demonstrate real interest in my work and have supported me at every turn along the way. I'd also like to thank the production editor, Bert Yaeger, who worked behind the scenes to coordinate the copy editing and pro-duction of my book. I couldn't get by in this business without my superb agent, Amy Rennert, and her assistant, Robyn Russell, who put the bug in my ear about switch-ing this to a first-person tale.

My writing pals buoy me up and share stories with me

about the writer's life, and make me believe I can do this. Rick Bragg is like kinfolk. William Gay and Tom Franklin, Suzanne Hudson, Joe Formichella, Bev Marshall and Jack Pendarvis, Cassandra King—they're all there for me.

And a book might as well be under a bushel basket without readers, who get their books with the help of booksellers and their incredible staffs, like John Evans's Lemuria Books, Richard Howorth's Square Books, Karin Wilson's Page and Palette, Scott Naugle's Pass Christian Books and Susan Daigre's Bookends (both stores were blown away by Katrina), Britton Trice's Garden District Bookstore, and Mary Gay Shipley's That Bookstore in Blytheville. Martin Lanaux took the reins at my Over the Transom Books and supplies me with anecdotes and reads my early drafts. Suzanne Barnhill keeps me humble with her fierce copy edits.

My friends Mac Walcott and David Poindexter and Smoky Davis never let me think this is all an illusion, and stand beside me in a real way. Cindy Saxon keeps me in the loop and makes sure the papers are shuffled and sent along on their right way. A long list of Fairhopers, from the grocery store and my kids' schools to the church and the coffeehouses, people who are kind and encouraging to me, all of you are essential to my writing.

Most important, members of my family, near and extended, put their faith in me in ways that completely energize my creative urges. Indeed, there's quite a crowd going along with me on this author's journey. Just hold the noise down, okay? We've got a scene to write.

About the Author

SONNY BREWER founded Over the
Transom Bookshop in Fairhope and is board
chairman of the nonprofit Fairhope Center
for the Writing Arts. He is the former editor
in chief of *Mobile Bay Monthly;* he also
published and edited *Eastern Shore Quarterly*
magazine, edited *Red Bluff Review,* and was
founding associate editor of the weekly
West Alabama Gazette. Brewer is also editor of
the acclaimed annual five-volume anthology
of Southern writing *Stories from the
Blue Moon Café* and author of
The Poet of Tolstoy Park.

About the Type

This book was set in Caslon, a typeface
first designed in 1722 by William Caslon.
Its widespread use by most English printers in
the early eighteenth century soon supplanted
the Dutch typefaces that had formerly
prevailed. The roman is considered a
"workhorse" typeface due to its pleasant,
open appearance, while the italic is
exceedingly decorative.